The Pen Pal Murders

James T. Falk

James Falk

SterlingHouse Publisher, Inc. Pittsburgh, PA

The Pen Pal Murders

PEMBERTON

PEMBERTON

ISBN 1-56315-388-2
9781563153884

Trade Paperback

Library of Congress #2007923558

Request for information should be addressed to:
SterlingHouse Publisher, Inc.
7436 Washington Avenue
Pittsburgh, PA 15218
www.sterlinghousepublisher.com

Pemberton Mysteries
is an imprint of SterlingHouse Publisher, Inc.

SterlingHouse Publisher, Inc. is a company
of the CyntoMedia Corporation

Cover Design: Brandon M. Bittner
Images Provided By: IStockphoto.com
Interior Design: N. J. McBeth

Printed in the United States of America

Dedicated to my son, Ben,
who cared and was very helpful

Chapter 1

Diane Duval paced nervously in front of the police station in downtown Pittsburgh. She never thought she'd ever need the police for anything, least of all to report a husband missing.

It was an imposing structure and it added to her nervousness. A late nineteenth-century behemoth, its walls were constructed of huge granite slabs. Twenty steps, protected at each end by reclining lions, spanned the width of the building. Four tall pillars at the top of the steps were carbon copies of those constructed by the Romans during Biblical times.

Diane took the first few steps for the third time and for the third time retreated to the sidewalk, still unsure about continuing. She wiped clammy palms on the side of her slacks. She had always found it difficult to understand her husband when he talked of having sweaty palms before an important presentation. Now she knew. There had to be many women who faced the same situation.

Husbands walk out on wives every day. Maybe other husbands had good reasons to do so, but she was sure that hers did not.

The place was busy. Men and women in blue uniforms and others in civilian clothes, many carrying briefcases, pushed in and out of a pair of non-stop revolving doors. She finally took a deep breath and hurried as fast as she could to the top of the steps.

Diane had never reported anything to the police — not even a phone complaint. If television programs were any criteria, the only experience she had with this kind of thing, she decided her visit would probably be met with a patronizing smile and a request to fill out an embarrassing report. Then, as the paper was plopped into a desk basket, she'd receive assurance that her husband, like so many others, would soon return home.

A few of her friends often went through the same thing. They even kidded about police getting to know them on a first-name basis. It was the only way they could retaliate, as meager as it was, against cheating husbands. Most of those women were up against a wall, not in a position to leave their husbands or file for a divorce, which Diane had suggested. After twelve years or so of marriage and maybe children, they were out of the job market. Even though a few like Diane had attended college or had degrees, technology passed them by. Unless they were willing to take some lesser job in favor of the comfort and income to which they were accustomed, there wasn't much else to do other than accept their fate. As she caught her breath at the top of the steps, Diane realized she might well have fallen into that category — a situation that had never before entered her mind.

In a husband's case, after whatever pleasures he sought, he headed home, resigned that the pleasures were well worth the abuse he could expect, along with bedroom denials. In most cases, denials were the cause of the problem. Diane felt that couldn't apply to her. There were no denials.

After virtually being pushed through the revolving doors, she stood in mild awe. The police station wasn't at all what she expected. People cast irritated glances as they veered right or left to pass her. Diane finally realized she was blocking traffic and quickly stepped aside after a woman bumped her and whispered, "Get the hell out of the way."

There was no narrow hallway or central room with the kind of activity she'd seen so many times on television police dramas. Instead, she was staring down a long, clean corridor that stretched the length of the building. Footsteps echoed as people hurried to whatever destinations. Instead of worn tongue-in-groove wood floors that Diane had expected, the floor was made of large granite squares embellished by elegant designs. Decorative patterns in the plaster ceiling, about thirty feet above, were almost indistinguishable due to a haze created by low-hanging florescent fixtures. The ceiling was probably beautiful in the days of incandescent lighting, she decided.

She had no idea where to go and started down the long passageway. Each office door window displayed painted lettering, Homicide Division, Criminal Division and Juvenile Division. Lettering on the final door read Media Lounge. As she neared it, a young woman, whom Diane assumed to be near her age, walked out. She carried a yellow legal tablet and was engrossed by whatever was written on it.

"Excuse me," Diane whispered, embarrassed to be interrupting the woman's concentration.

The woman looked over a shoulder and realized Diane was talking to her. "Can I help you?"

Diane took a deep breath. After a moment of hesitation, she asked if there was a missing persons office.

"Missing? Who's missing?" The woman sensed the possible story.

"My husband," Diane whispered.

"Oh," the woman uttered. There was an understanding smile as she pointed her tablet toward the other end of the hallway. "The first door on the left."

Diane called after her, thanking her for the help, but got no response. "I guess missing husbands are old hat around here," she muttered as she retraced her steps. When she entered the building, Diane had turned her attention first to the right and by the time she looked left, she had already passed the missing persons office.

The room was drab. The walls were dull yellow, the furniture metal gray. A long counter separated two desks from the front door. A picture of Pittsburgh's mayor hung above a row of wood filing cabinets. Duplicates hung in every city office. Diane was tired of seeing his face, especially since she voted for his opponent.

Cracks disappeared at the top of its frame and reappeared at the bottom. Flanking the cabinets were flags, one of the United States, the other of the state.

An officer at one of the desks was paunchy and older than other policemen she'd seen in the hall and outside. She felt a bit more at ease as she noticed three stripes on his sleeves. She knew he was a sergeant. Her husband had been a sergeant in the Marine Corps and she knew they were at least somewhat important.

"Ma'am," he answered after she explained the situation, "husbands stray every day. Some wives do, too. You might not believe it, but police get tons of complaints every day about gallivanting spouses." He shook his head, took a deep breath, and plopped some papers he was carrying into a desk basket. "Didn't you call your precinct station? That's where you should have gone. They could've handled it."

"I did call."

"And?"

"They didn't want to help."

"They what? Who said they wouldn't?"

"Well, nobody actually said they didn't want to help. But they did say there was nothing they could do. They told me to come back in a day or two if he didn't return. It seems like that's just about the same as saying they weren't going to help. They didn't seem too concerned."

"And?"

"And what? Sergeant, I know my husband. He had no business trips scheduled. He had no reason to stay away like this."

"Oh?" the man replied, tilting his head and raising an eyebrow as he surveyed Diane's body — at least the part that showed above the counter. He gave a mild, approving nod that irritated her. "Maybe so, but you'd also be surprised at how many wives, almost as ... ah as pretty as you, tell the same story every day."

"I really don't give much of a damn what other women look like or say or do. My husband is missing and I need help."

The man extended his arms, palms outward as a gesture for Diane to calm down.

"Since when?"

"That's more like it. Last night, after work."

"Last night? That's only twelve or so hours ago."

"I can tell time. He's been missing for that long."

The man stood, took another deep breath, stretched his arms, and laid his hands, palms down, on the counter.

"We can't do anything here. This is a precinct matter and you'll have to get with them tomorrow."

Diane mimicked him. She stretched her arms and placed her hands, palms down on the counter. He backed off a bit. She glared at him for a few quiet seconds.

"Jeesus, do you all rehearse the same stupid lines?"

"Sounds sort of like it, doesn't it?" He chuckled. "We care, lady. We really do, but there are procedures. First of all, we can't take complaints or inquiries here from people from all over the city. Good lord, we'd be swamped in a day." He held a hand 12 inches or so above the counter, simulating an imaginary stack of papers.

"Did you check everywhere — where he works, the bars he goes to?"

"No. I just came down here to pass the time of day with you."

"Listen, Mrs. Duval, I'm doing the best I can to advise you. Think what you like." He started toward his desk.

"I'm sorry. Yes, I checked everywhere. His secretary said he was leaving for home when she last talked to him, and he doesn't stop off at bars. And if he goes out, it's usually with somebody from his office or me."

"Okay. What does he look like and what's his full name?"

"Ronald Duval." Diane then described her husband in full detail.

"Wait here. I'll check the accident reports from this area that came in last night. Does your husband have a cell phone?"

"I never get an answer. It must be turned off or dead."

The man left and returned in five minutes and shook his head.

She had already discounted an accident. If there had been one, somebody would have called by then after looking at his identification cards.

"Nope. Nothing. No report on anyone fitting your husband's description, but something could be in one of our precincts."

"Wouldn't someone have notified me after looking at his driver's license or other cards?"

"What if his wallet was lost? What if it was stolen? That happens a lot. There are a lot of people out there who would rob pennies from their dead mother's eyes. Maybe he was arrested."

Diane hadn't thought of that.

"Well, anyhow, I'm having a man send a notice out with your husband's description to all precincts. They'll contact you if there is anything. That's the best I can do. Meanwhile, I think you'd better go home and wait for him. He just might be there right now worrying about where you are. That's probably it."

"Can't you put out some kind of bulletin right now?"

"Ma'am, can you even begin to imagine how many bulletins we'd be putting out every day for everyone who's missing? I'm telling you — and this if from years of experience — they always show up and so will your husband." He moved back behind his desk as he spoke. It was his way of indicating that the conversation was over.

"You think he's just out screwing around."

"I didn't say that, and I am sorry, but there isn't much I can do right now. Not much anyone can do, until tomorrow at least." With that, he picked up a stack of papers from the desk, gave Diane one last apologetic look, told her not to worry, her husband would be back, then retreated through the rear door.

Diane stood for a few moments outside the entrance to the room. Another woman brushed past and hurried into the office.

Poor thing, Diane said to herself. She'll get the same line. She took another deep breath. "Now what do I do?"

Chapter 2

There wasn't much Diane could do other than follow the man's advice: go home and wait. The drive took an unusually long time, especially for early afternoon. Actually, the delay was her fault. Her mind wasn't on driving, but on the disappearance of her husband and the reluctance of anyone to do anything about it. She knew she was driving below the posted speed, but was oblivious to the sound of horns, flashing headlights and the physical signs of anger and frustration. Most Pittsburgh streets are hilly and narrow, especially in the South Hills where she lived, and nobody was able to pass her. None of that bothered her.

Her only thought was that her husband's car might be in the driveway. It wasn't. She rested her head against the headrest and stared at the car's ceiling. Finally, she released a long sigh, wiped tears from her cheeks and started for the house. The phone rang as she approached the door.

She fumbled frantically with her keys, finally found the right one and slipped it into place. By then, the phone had rung four or five times and she tripped over a floor lamp in her desperation to answer it.

"Ron is that you? Where are you?"

She recognized the voice of Marie, her husband's secretary, collapsed onto her sofa, and struggled to keep from falling apart.

"I was calling about Mr. Duval. He was supposed to make a presentation this afternoon. Is he ill?"

"No, he isn't sick." Diane's voice was unsteady and tapered off to a whisper with her last words. "He isn't here." After several moments of uncomfortable silence, Diane cleared her throat and continued, her voice still not much above a whisper.

"I mean, he never did get home yesterday."

"He didn't call?"

"There's no trace. You told me he was on his way home. He always comes right home or calls if he can't."

"He said nothing about going anywhere. He said goodnight, see you tomorrow, and there was nothing to indicate that anything was out of the ordinary."

"Well he didn't make it," Diane said.

"I'm sure he'll get in touch with you. We were worried because he never misses this kind of meeting. We thought maybe he had a problem on his way in."

"I've checked everywhere," Diane said, "including hospitals last night and the police this morning. Nothing in the hospitals and all the police said is wait for a while and he'll be back. They insisted that he's out screwing around. I guess they hear the same story so many times they've become immune to it. If the President was reported missing in Pittsburgh, they'd probably tell the Secret Service that he's up in the Hill District screwing around, and that he'll be back."

There was a slight nervous chuckle followed by a few more long moments of silence.

"Just hang in there," Marie said. Apparently, she couldn't think of much else to say. "You'll call if you hear anything?"

Diane assured her and lowered the phone back into its cradle. She'd just have to wait. That wasn't anything new. She waited for many things in her lifetime — parties, gifts, trips, waiting for Ron to propose, and now waiting for Ron to call or to find out if he was even alive. Diane never experienced anxiety that would come close to approaching this. She tried a to rid her mind of the myriad things she imagined could have happened, but nothing worked.

She tried a magazine, then the radio, and then television. She remembered reading about a person who turned on the radio and heard that a loved one had been killed in an accident. She remembered, too, of reading about a woman in Detroit who, while driving home, heard a news report about a shooting in her neighborhood. When she arrived, two of her brothers were dead. That possibility had run through Diane's mind several times and in some warped, even morbid manner, she wished some kind of newsflash would occur. At least she'd know something. She found herself continuously changing stations, not really remembering what she heard last, but subconsciously hoping for some word, good or bad.

Diane decided to call her parents. She had the phone in her hand and even began dialing, but then decided for the time being against calling any family member. She knew what the responses would be from both sides. And she could avoid that headache, since she expected Ron to be back.

According to her doting and protective mother, Ron was a spoiled brat and not good enough for Diane. All Diane could expect were some choice "I told you so," comments. The immediate attitude of Ron's parents would probably be that he had finally wised up and left, although outwardly they would probably console Diane. The Duvals were country club people and Diane's family wasn't. Ron's parents had others in mind for him, and Diane wasn't even in the running. What both sets of parents failed to realize was that Diane and Ron cared little about what they thought.

Diane decided to wait just a little longer. She felt she could avoid that headache, since she expected Ron to come back. Her mother and in-laws could never have to know what happened.

By early evening, Diane was back in her car, driving through her neighborhood, sobbing as she drove. She remembered years before, as a six-year-old, how she had cried as her father drove for hours searching for her dog. They never found it, and she never had another one. She didn't ever want to go through that pain again. The thought of never finding Ron, or of his never returning, was so overpowering and she had to pull off the road several times.

Her search expanded to more distant neighborhoods, criss-crossing each block in a frantic search that grew more frenzied with each disappointment.

Occasionally her heart rate increased as she approached a car like Ron's, only to suffer a bitter disappointment. Each moment of hope was followed by minutes of anger and then despair. She felt sure he wouldn't be with another woman, but she still could not shake the thought. As a result, she extended her search to the parking lots of every bar and motel within a few miles of their home. She knew that was a waste of time. If Ron was with another woman, they'd certainly be at some distant and remote spot. After three hours, she finally gave up and headed for home.

She had made sure the answering machine was on when she left and prayed as she unlocked the door that the red light would be flashing. It was.

"Oh, please," she cried aloud, as she fumbled with the phone and pushed the recorder play button.

The voice was strange. She didn't recognize it. It was low and soft. It was almost intimate, yet somehow menacing. There were only a few words.

"Diane. This is your pen pal. I'll be visiting soon."

"Who is this?" she asked, trying to keep from panicking or yelling. Then she realized that she was talking to a recording and banged the receiver down so heavily that it bounced out of its cradle and dangled over the end of the table.

"What the hell is going on?" she cried out, and immediately called the police from a phone in her bedroom. She was assured it was probably someone who knew the situation, possibly from where Ron worked. They didn't think she'd get any more calls. "There isn't much more we can do with calls like that," she was told.

Diane picked up the jacket and keys she had dropped when she stumbled in her haste to get to the phone. She tossed the jacket across a nearby chair, dropped the keys on her coffee table and collapsed across her sofa.

Chapter 3

Sleep was out of the question. Every time she heard a car approach, she'd stumble to the window, only to watch dejectedly as the car's taillights disappeared. No matter how many times she tried to stop, at the next sound she rushed back to the window.

It was worse than the first night, and as much as she didn't want to think about it, the police sergeant may have been right. Whatever Ron was up to, she knew he would be back, perhaps in a condition in which she'd never seen him before, but he would be back.

Diane considered every possibility. Ron was murdered. He was kidnapped for a ransom, since Ron's parents were very wealthy. Maybe he ran off with another woman or a man. Nothing was beyond the realm of imagination, and Diane's was working overtime.

Scenarios of each possibility repeatedly ran through her mind. He might have been robbed and murdered and his body dumped into a ditch. And she still couldn't shake visualizations of what he might be doing at that moment with another person. She was dead tired and emotionally drained, but there was no way of stopping what her imagination was conjuring up. Her mind even provided the images with faces of people they knew.

Diane had read, mostly in women's magazines, that many wives know why their husbands leave, but they kid themselves, even lie about it. Most of it has to do with money or sex — or the lack thereof. As far as Diane was concerned, those were the least of the reasons for her husband wanting to leave.

Ron had an excellent job, and, as far as sex was concerned, that was no problem. Diane felt they had an excellent relationship, a bit kinky sometimes, but solid. To think of her husband doing the same with someone else was unacceptable. Her imagination continued to create new situations, and she became more upset with each. The whole thing was incongruous. She loved Ron. She was worried sick and wanted him back. But at the same time, she was beginning to hate him for what he was putting her through.

Diane forgot about going to bed. In a matter of minutes she'd be back to the window. Instead, she went to the living room and flopped heavily upon the sofa. She leaned over; head drooped, forearms resting against her thighs, trying to make some sense out of the situation. She sat upright and spoke as though someone was there, listening. She flailed her arms and hands as one might do when totally frustrated.

"Damn, this is stupid. If he wants to take off, if he wants to shack up with some broad, why should I sit here like an idiot and worry myself to death?"

She picked up a magazine and lay down, determined to get involved with one of the articles. It didn't work. She read, but it was futile. Sentences massed into garbled phrases that had no meaning and finally, pages faded into solid blurs.

Diane was aware of the magazine slipping from her grasp, aware that she was dozing off, and even as she did, she wondered how long it would be before another sound would have her back up.

It could have been minutes or an hour before the ringing of the phone awakened her. For a few seconds she couldn't even remember where she was. She fumbled for the receiver.

"Hello," she whispered, eyes closed, hoping for the familiar voice. Nobody spoke, but she knew someone was on the line.

"Good lord, Ron, if that's you, damn it, say something!"

There was still no reply. After a few seconds, she heard a barely audible click.

"Damn, damn, damn!" She flung the already damaged phone hard to the floor. It shattered. She pressed her hands to the side of her head. Her voice, low like a dog's quiet whimper, increased to a horrendous and long scream. She buried her face into the pillow, muffling the sound, and pounded the sofa with both fists. She cried herself back to sleep.

Whenever the sofa creaked as she moved, it would awaken her. She remembered times before, strange moments when she dreamed and was suddenly awakened, and how she could quickly close her eyes and the dream would return exactly where it had left off. She tried it.

Ron was once again beside her. She reached for him and though he appeared to be close, she was unable to touch him. She'd open her eyes, see the shadows in the room, close them, and Ron would be there. Then he began to drift away.

She called his name, frantically reaching out, but still unable to touch him. His last words, the only words that were discernible as his image faded, were, "I'm dead."

Diane screamed his name as she struggled to sit up. She was drenched in perspiration. She leaned forward, hands cupped over her face, barely muffling involuntary gasps.

She stumbled from the sofa into the bathroom and splashed cold water on her face. The reflection in the mirror was barely recognizable. The look of horror, fright, and panic was one she could have never duplicated on purpose.

"Good lord, I'm going crazy," she screamed at the image in the mirror. She took another deep breath, toweled her face and headed for the kitchen. A cup of coffee didn't help, and she couldn't shake thinking of the dream and the only words that were clear.

How many times had she read where dreams were manifestations of one's thoughts, desires, fantasies or fears, but most times in a non-sensible way. Her greatest fear was that her husband 'was' dead and so he ended up in a dream telling her so.

Chapter 4

"Sergeant Thomas here."

Diane could hardly remember dialing, or even getting back to the bedroom where the only workable phone remained. She almost hung up, too embarrassed to continue. She muttered a few unintelligible words before clearing her throat.

"What's that?"

Diane was almost whispering. "Sergeant, my name is Diane Duval. My husband has been missing now for several days. I'm calling to see if you might have had any word of anything involving him. His name is Ronald Duval."

"No, ma'am," the sergeant answered.

The quick response surprised Diane. *How could he know that fast? They're pulling my leg again.*

"Goddard, from downtown, sent a notice to all precincts about your husband. I'll tell you lady, that's not done often, especially by him, not for a missing husband. He gets them all day long. But he said you seemed to be one of the few women who report missing husbands for something more serious than a family feud. He is concerned. Come in. Ask for me."

Diane thanked him. She felt better, but only for a while, until she began to think again about possible reasons for her husband's disappearance. There was the possibility of embezzlement at work, or maybe an accident where his car might be hidden in one of Pittsburgh's deep roadside ravines, or possibly amnesia. But like all the other times, she couldn't shake the idea of his being with somebody else.

Diane liked sex, and she wasn't afraid to try anything, and neither was her husband. So the physical part of their relationship — at least to her, was ideal and open. She knew she was more than just pretty. A person knew where they rated on a beauty scale of one to ten, Diana thought, and Diane knew she was high. Because of that, the idea of another woman hurt.

She often fantasized about other men and what they might be like, and she was sure Ron thought likewise about other women. There wasn't a person in the world who didn't think of such things, she was sure. But that was as far as her fantasies went. Evidently, she decided, Ron's went further.

The precinct police station was closer to what she had expected. It was six or seven stories, square and constructed of weather-beaten red bricks. The windows on an upper floor were barred. She supposed that was where prisoners were held. A short flight of concrete steps with black iron railings led to heavy double doors. Above them was a timeworn slab with engraved gothic lettering that read: "Precinct No. Eight, 1932". The building wasn't as foreboding as the one downtown.

Diane knew there would be speculation about her relationship with her husband. What was she really like? Hot? Cold? Was she a nagger? Was she unfaithful? Her husband was gone, and there had to be reasons for him to walk out. Each person would choose his or her own theory, and with each repetition there would be embellishment. Soon, Diane Duval would be he star of the neighborhood soap.

If she wasn't beautiful, she was exceptionally attractive, what some might call model pretty, girlish and enticing. No matter if she were clad in a beautiful evening gown or in blue jeans, she was the kind of woman who could cause a guy to have a sexual experience as they passed each in a building or on the street. Diane's hair was pitch black, her eyes green. She was tall — five-nine or so, and slender, and her long legs accentuated close to perfect thighs and hips. Her breasts were not big, but not small. Ron was envied, and his friends often reminded him how lucky he was to have a woman like her.

She had no doubt that there would be juicy opinions. She knew, because she and Ron were guilty of the same thing when a couple they knew broke up. She was worse than Ron. He usually let it go after a few minutes of speculation, but Diane always let her imagination run wild. It was fun, envisioning an indiscretion. She never was involved in one, so thinking about it, envisioning one, even with someone they knew, was like a game to her. Sometime she wondered if she'd ever make it more. She could only imagine what it was going to be like when everyone else did find out.

Once inside the building, she had no idea where to go. The hall was crowded. Some people were standing while others occupied benches that lined the walls. There were men and women of all ages. Some appeared to be destitute; others were attired in very expensive outfits. She pushed her way past the crowd and hurried through the first door she came to. The setting may have been every day routine for those inside, but Diane found it almost impossible to separate the bad guys and the good guys, they looked so much alike. She was able to decide on some by who was pushing or being pushed.

Every desk was cluttered and most of them were occupied. Some people were standing and arguing. Eventually, they were shoved into seats, subdued and even threatened by men whose bearded faces were no more than a foot from theirs. She heard the words "police brutality" shouted out at least a dozen times, but nobody paid much attention.

There were characters with clipboards and coffee cups, so familiar to Diane from her TV and movie experiences. Ringing of phones added to the cacophony. She looked for anyone who might be a lawyer. None fit her description, and Diane presumed the room might have been off limits to anyone but police and those arrested. Then she remembered, again via TV, that lawyers, police or prosecutors and those arrested had special rooms in which to meet.

Finally a bearded man dressed in worn clothing approached her. He scrutinized her from head to toe.

"Wow! Whom do you belong to?"

Diane eyed him coolly, not sure what, or who he was.

"I don't belong to anybody. I'm looking for Sergeant Thomas."

The man rubbed the stubble on his chin and eyed her up and down for a few more uncomfortable moments.

"Lucky guy, lady, but you're looking in the wrong place. He's up a floor. How'd you get into this room in the first place?"

She nodded toward the door. "How do you think? It doesn't take much intelligence to figure that out, does it?

The man smiled and nodded, then shrugged his shoulders.

"I guess so. That's probably why I'm an undercover man. I fit right in with the generally low street mentality, but at least I can read." He nodded toward the door.

Diane followed his glance. The words: "Do Not Enter" in large, bold lettering, showed backwards through the glass. She was in such a hurry to get through the crowd that she hadn't bothered to read the printing.

"You waltzed right past the check-in counter. Anyhow, I'll take you to him." He bowed, waved an open palm toward the door, and followed her. She knew he had to be making some kind of gestures behind her back, judging from the remarks and subdued catcalls that attended their progress. She was glad to get out of there.

The room they entered was just the opposite from that which they left. It was relatively quiet, with maybe a half dozen men and women in plain cloths at desks. A secretary was stationed just inside the door. Diane was led to one of the desks.

"Sarge, lady here to see ya." He winked at Diane, gave another quick approving check of her body, and left.

The man stood and motioned her to a chair beside his desk. A woman nearby was writing on a note pad.

"I'm Bob Thomas."

Diane introduced herself. She nodded toward the woman, thinking she was first in line.

"I'm just checking some of last night's action," the woman said.

Diane recognized her as the person who had given her directions at the central police station. Diane looked from the woman to Thomas. She did not want the reporter to hear what she had to say. Thomas knew what Diane had to be thinking and smiled.

"She's all right, a news reporter."

Diane sat silently for a few seconds, head slightly lowered. "What now?" she finally whispered.

"Well, first of all, I'll get you some java and we'll see what we can do." He started toward a rear door. "Black? Sugar?"

"Doesn't matter."

"Was the day I met you the first day your husband was missing?" the reporter asked.

Surprised, Diane was not sure that she should even answer, but did anyway. "Yes."

"Did he ever leave before?"

"No." Diane wished the woman would mind her own business.

"My name's Marge Bennett." She sensed there might be something beyond a thoughtless or cheating husband. Their wives don't usually end up talking to detectives.

Diane shrugged and the reporter went quietly back to taking notes, but she was listening.

Thomas handed the coffee to Diane. It tasted good even though she never used cream or sugar. "Thank you," she whispered.

"What's a coffee?"

"No. I meant for your interest."

"Oh, that. It's my job. Anyway, Goddard — that's the sergeant you spoke to downtown — thought you seemed a bit different from most of the others."

They sipped the brew, then Thomas continued.

"Mrs. Duval, I want you to do something that can be very trying. But it's a must and I hope you're up to it."

"Up to what?"

"I'm going to take you back downtown for a look at several bodies in the morgue. They were brought in over the last couple days. There was no identification on some of them."

"Oh, God." Diane slumped against the back of the chair. She closed her eyes and dropped her chin almost to her chest while slowly shaking her head. "I thought you said there was nothing."

"Well, they don't seem to fit your husband's description, but it's the only way we can be sure. If you'd rather wait, we can."

"If he's there, what good would waiting do?"

"Would you mind very much if I met you there?" Bennett asked.

It surprised Diane. "Why?"

"I don't know. Couldn't help but to be interested. By now, it seems your husband should have been back."

Diane knew the rest of the unspoken explanation — 'unless something has happened to him.'

"How could this be interesting to you, if it's a missing husband who everybody thinks is out screwing around?"

"Mainly because it sounds a bit different and I'm a reporter; police beat, and all the trash that goes with it."

"I don't think my situation is trash, or anything that goes with it." Diane turned again to Thomas for support.

Bennett answered before he could say anything. "You're right, and I am sorry for the bad choice of words. I won't interfere. I promise."

Very little was said during the trip to downtown. The morgue was cold, not temperature cold, but barren cold. The particular part they were visiting was nothing more than a long, sterile, white-walled corridor. It was lined on both sides with three by three foot square metal doors, two high.

Diane recalled the time many years before when she and several teenage friends visited the former morgue on Fourth Avenue. It was a challenge just to go in, and she remembered pushing each other to see who would venture first. They also had walked down a similar aisle. Instead of single pullout cubicles, there were aisle-long glass enclosed refrigerated cases on each side. They were much like those used in markets to display meat products. Each row contained tilted slabs on which bodies, covered to their chins with white sheets, were displayed. She remembered some, whose half-opened, dull eyed, seemed to stare directly at her. Diane closed her eyes as the man pulled a gurney from the vault and removed the sheet from the face of the first corpse.

"Mrs. Duval."

She forced herself to look. The face was ghastly chalk gray, eyes barely open, exactly as the faces appeared years before. Diane's chest felt as though it was in a vice. She had difficulty breathing. "No," she whispered. Bennett held her by an arm as the attendant pulled another gurney from a vault.

The process was repeated several more times, and it didn't get any easier. With each "no" came the probability that the next one would be a "yes". Finally the ordeal was over. Her husband was not among the dead.

An hour later they were back at the precinct. The reporter rode with them, leaving her car behind. It was a smart news hawk ploy, since it would leave Diane with no option but to drive Bennett back to the morgue, giving her more time for prying. Thomas handed each of the women a cup of coffee.

"I know it was more than difficult, but the good news is that your husband was not there."

Diane nodded.

"But you may have to go through the same thing again, maybe even a couple times."

"I hope not," Diane said. "But there is something else."

Thomas tilted his head a bit and raised his eyebrows.

Diane told him about the phone calls. They didn't seem to bother Thomas. He asked Diane about their acquaintances, and then surprised her by asking if anyone tried to come on to her.

"A number of times."

"It may seem a bit strange, but calls like that are rather common in the situation in which you find yourself. Somebody you've rebuffed, or somebody with a weird imagination might think of it as a prank, or a way to get even for being spurned."

"Or it just could be some demented weirdo," Bennett interjected.

Thomas took a long sip of coffee. "Who knows about this other than us?"

"I don't see how anyone could. You, Miss Bennett here, and those where Ron works are the only ones. I'm not sure how many there even know of it."

Thomas gave Diane's hand an assuring squeeze.

"Well, it's obvious that somebody does, so let us work on that angle, too. I'll call you as soon as we get or hear anything,"

Diane had barely reached the bottom of the station steps when Bennett called her. "Can you give me a lift?"

How could she refuse?

"Mrs. Duval," the reporter said as they walked toward the car, "can we spend a bit of time together?"

"Why? What can you do?"

"Probably nothing, but I will treat you to lunch when we get down town. I'm sure you don't feel like going home right away, and it might be nice just to have someone to talk to."

Chapter 5

After the loneliness since Ron was gone, Diane welcomed the opportunity. She liked downtown Pittsburgh. While other big cities were dying, Pittsburgh seemed to be almost as vibrant as it was when she was a child. And according to her parents, it had changed little since they were younger. But that was a bit of nostalgic exaggeration.

"Strictly Italian," Bennett said as she held open the door of the narrow-fronted restaurant. "I eat here a lot. They have great pasta, and if you're not real hungry, there are tasty meatball sandwiches, and at reporters' wages. It's the best of its kind in town."

"Sounds good," Diane answered as Bennett led the way to a corner booth. "Funny, I never noticed this place before."

"Well," Bennett said, "it's on the busiest street in Pittsburgh, but it seems to be out of the way."

The restaurant was quaint and reminded Diane of those one might see in an old gangster flick; wood floor, an antiquated decorative tin-plate ceiling probably installed during the Depression years, slowly rotating ceiling fans, red leather cushioned booths and square four-chair tables with traditional old country red checkered cloths.

Diane slid into the booth. "Nice. I feel like I should be expecting a bomb to come flying through the window."

Bennett laughed. "I had the same feeling the first time I came here. Actually, this is as close to that Roaring Twenties decor as anything around. I've chatted with old-timers who swear this place was a hangout for mobsters during prohibition." Bennett pointed to photos on the wall.

"Some places have photos of athletes or movie stars on their walls, so Tony, the owner, got into the swing of things, except he hung photos of gangsters all over the place, and surprisingly, it didn't seem to offend anybody. His family has had Italian restaurants, including this one, since those Prohibition days."

As they chatted, a short, robust man with a small white towel draped over his left arm approached. His shirt was white; trousers and bowtie black. His face was pudgy, nose wide, lips heavy, and his skin reflected some childhood pox. He still had a full crop of black hair, not a sign of gray. It matched heavy eyebrows. His accent complimented his appearance and the house decor perfectly.

"Hey, Margie, my a little bambina, how a ya doin'?" The man was apparently in his seventies and definitely old country Italian. "When are you gonna write another story about my place?"

"When you decide to serve good food," Bennett said mimicking the old man's accent.

She introduced Diane. They shook hands and Tony turned his attention back to Bennett.

Diane thought how much Ron would like the restaurant. Maybe he had already been there. He loved good Italian food. Ron grew up in a Pittsburgh suburb heavily populated by Italian families. He often talked about the great friendships, greater pasta dinners, and stealing and "cutting" homemade red wine with ginger ale when he and his friends were kids. For a few moments, Diane had forgotten that he had even disappeared.

Bennett sensed a mood change and quickly ordered.

"Tony, give us each one of those beautiful meatball sandwiches and a couple light drafts."

Bennett tapped the table for a few seconds before continuing.

"You know, I've been coming here since I started at the *Press* — that's twelve years and I didn't learn Tony's last name until three years ago. That's when I did a feature story on this place and his family. The name also reminded me of a James Cagney type gangster movie. Okay, Mr. Napolitano, take this. Bang! Bang!"

They both laughed.

"Bad acting," Diane said. "It is a shame, though, that Italians were always portrayed as the bad guys."

"But that was Pittsburgh. New York and Chicago were far worse. They were always persecuted, so they only had one way to go. Blacks talk about being persecuted, but not any worse than Italians, Irish and especially Chinese and Indians. The latter two were like buffalo in the old west, shot for sport."

More awkward silence followed before Bennett decided to get to what she considered the subject matter.

"I can only imagine how you must feel."

"Rotten, and that's putting it mildly."

"It might do you some good to talk about it a bit."

Diane didn't answer and Bennett let it go.

The food arrived and they ate, for the most part in silence, broken only by a bit of idle talk or when Bennett chatted with colleagues as they passed the table.

Diane knew there would be questions sooner or later, and maybe Marge Bennett was right. It might be good just to loosen up a bit. Marge ordered a second round. Diane couldn't remember when she had her last glass of beer, let alone two. But it did have a warming effect.

"I feel like having a dozen of these." Diane lifted the glass a few inches. "It might help me out of my misery."

"Wouldn't help. I've tried that. The hangover's worse than the problem. You know, the mysterious calls intrigue me. I'm sure Thomas will come up with some explanation." Bennett took long sips before continuing. "You did say this was the first time you've had calls like you described."

Diane nodded. "And for no reason that I can think of."

"No other woman?" Bennett hurriedly continued. "I think I can ask that because, even though I'm not married, I lost my man to another woman and it tore me up."

"Well, this is doing the same to me."

"How long have you been married?"

"A little over ten years — nineteen eighty-two." Diane twisted a napkin as she continued. "They say after ten years is about the time a lot of husbands start scouting around."

"Women, too, but everybody has a 'they say', and I never have believed in a 'they say'. You happily married?"

"I always thought so."

"Where'd you meet?"

"College."

"Oh?"

"We met at Pitt. I majored in physical education program. I wanted to enroll at Slippery Rock. It's said to have the best physical ed major, but my parents said the name was funny, and decided on the University of Pittsburgh. That was rather stupid, I thought, but they were footing the bill. I was lucky that I did go there or I would have never met Ron."

"Did he ...." Bennett quickly corrected herself. "Does he have a good job?"

"Very good. Ron majored in communication and went into that field."

"Family?"

"No. We lost two babies, miscarriages, and decided not to put me through that anymore. Had my tubes tied. We often thought about adopting. As a matter of fact, we had planned to start the process in about a month."

"That sure doesn't sound like a situation where either party was ready to fly the coop."

"No, it doesn't, and that's why this is so perplexing."

Bennett took a long sip, looked over the rim of the glass and fingered its stem as she posed the next question. "What do you think?"

"I think something's happened to him. I mean something really bad."

"Why do you say that?"

"Because he never left before, not like this."

"Well, I never suspected my boyfriend when he was away, but when he was away, it was time to play. And then one day he, too, was gone. The only difference was that the next day he called, told me what was going down and that he would pick up his things while I was at work. I hated him, and I think I still do. Four years of my life were gone — poof, like that." Bennett emphasized the point by snapping her fingers.

"So you think my husband could have someone on the side and is now ready for the" — Diane snapped her fingers — "poof."

"Well again, what do you think?"

"I don't think that at all. He's dead. I know it."

"You know what? Why? How?"

"I dreamt it."

"You dreamt it?" Bennett smiled.

"Yes. Is that so funny?"

"No. But that probably was just your mind working overtime. Did your dream indicate how he died?"

"No. He just told me he was dead."

"Your husband told you that he was dead."

"Yes."

Bennett took a deep breath and leaned back against the cushion. "Wow. This is really different. I hope he was wrong."

"I don't think he was. I don't think he was cheating, so what other reason could there be for his disappearance? I trusted him."

"The same reason that brought most of those other women to the stations."

"Just because your boyfriend cheated on you don't mean all men do the same."

"You're right." Bennett spun her glass slowly around, clucked her tongue and continued. "So, how are we going to find out what has happened to your husband?"

"We? Not we. Where'd you ever get that idea? It's me. You don't have to worry about it. I'll find out."

She thought that would be the end of it, but Bennett persisted.

"Look Diane, if you really think that something bad has happened, then I'd like to help."

"Might be a good story?"

"I wasn't thinking of that, but anytime someone disappears, I mean into thin air, certainly there's story potential."

"But you see, I don't need your help."

"Yes you do, only you won't admit it."

"Well, if and when I do need help, there are always private detectives as well as the police."

"Oh yes, but the former are expensive and the latter won't do much unless there's a body."

Diane started out of the booth. Bennett restrained her.

"Look. I'm not trying to be funny. And I'm not just interested in working up a story either. I really do want to help. We have something in common. If your husband is alive, that means we've both been dumped. If not, then someone has to find out what happened and what this caller wants with you, although I can guess."

Diane leaned heavily on the table and glared at Bennett. "What the hell do you mean, dumped? We were married and in love. We were not shacking up for four years, where whomever got tired of the other first could pack up and bug out. You have a lot of damned nerve."

"I'm sorry. It was a bad choice of words."

"Damned right it was."

"Will you at least call me if your husband doesn't come back?"

"I'll call the police, not you. You're getting the jobs mixed up. They search. You write."

"Yes. I write, but I also know how to search. And sometimes I do it better than the police."

"I'll try to remember that."

Diane started up again. Bennett apologized again and asked her to stay.

"No. You stay. Have another on me." Diane fumbled through her purse and tossed a ten-dollar bill on the table. "There must be better stories in Pittsburgh than a missing husband."

"Not if he's dead, as you seem to think. I meant it when I said I'm sorry, but I still want to help you."

Diane didn't answer.

"Naive," Bennett muttered as she watched Diane push through the doors and disappear past the front window.

Chapter 6

As Diane drove home, she was tormented by the thought that if her husband were dead with no trace of his whereabouts, there would never be a funeral, or funeral home, or flowers. He'd just be gone, and a huge part of her life would be dispatched into another dimension, as though her husband had never existed.

Or, if he were in fact, with another person, he'd still be gone out of her life, but on her own volition. She'd see to that. She was already beginning to feel detached. But her mind still played games.

It was Ron, not her, who walked out. It was Ron, not her, who was probably with someone else. And it was Ron, not her, who apparently thought little, if anything at all, of the passion and love that had been part of their lives. Maybe it wasn't important to him, but it was to her.

Diane decided, as she maneuvered through traffic, that Marge Bennett might have been right. Ron dumped her. And if that were the case, then she wouldn't spend much time worrying and wondering what she did wrong.

"There it is," she said out loud, "just like they say, the wife starts blaming herself. I'm wondering what I did wrong."

But as she turned onto her street, the posturing she had made while driving vanished. There was no way to avoid the anticipation of Ron's car being in the driveway, and the bitter disappointment when it wasn't.

As she walked toward her front door, she glanced toward the direction from where Ron usually came. They sometimes arrived at the same time, but Ron's car didn't appear. Then she looked in the other direction. Not there either, but she did notice a black sedan parked halfway down the block. It was one she had never before seen in her immediate neighborhood. While she continued to stare, the car eased around the corner and disappeared. Probably someone dropped off a friend, she decided.

Her glance automatically went to the answering machine as she entered the house. No blinking light. Another disappointment. Several minutes later she was pouring a cup of coffee and should have been doing the same for Ron. Only after she'd poured her own did she realize that she had subconsciously set two places.

She remembered that, as a child, she had an imaginary friend, Cindy, to talk to. When Diane was upset or had been scolded, she would confide in Cindy, and Cindy always listened and was always sympathetic. She recalled how she would place a play cup of milk across the table, just as she had placed the coffee cup. And she would pour out her young soul. Soon the milk would be gone. Diane would drink both glasses, but in her young, imaginative mind, Cindy drank her own. She wished she could bring Cindy back. She was always so comforting.

Diane always loved Ron. She was worried about Ron, but since he could be gone forever, she was also worried about herself and her future. She felt somewhat ashamed, almost selfish, thinking that way, especially when his last words to her were that he loved her.

"If it's another woman, then for God's sake, tell me."

She then realized that she was standing and hovering over the table, talking at an empty cup, as though Ron were sitting behind it. She was about to sit back down when the phone rang. It startled her and she spilled coffee over her blouse as she hurried to answer it.

"Hello," she answered, her voice bristling with anticipation.

There was no response.

She repeated herself.

Still no answer.

"Ron, is that you?"

Silence.

"Listen, whoever you are. Why are you doing this to me and what have you done to my husband?"

A few seconds of silence passed,

"Diane, you'll find out in due time."

Then the line went dead.

"Damn you," Diane shouted. She knew the caller was gone, but the hurt and frustration were overpowering. She slumped onto the sofa, buried her head in her hands and cried. It was the onset of another long and lonely night.

A book or magazine would be out of the question. She'd tried those before. The television lasted but a few minutes. Diane searched both daily papers, thoroughly scanning each page for any article that had anything to do with an accident, murder or an unidentified body in Pittsburgh, or any other city. It wasn't until near midnight before she was emotionally and physically drained enough to be able to sleep and that was only after a long period of tossing and turning.

Diane was awakened a few hours later by the sound of a car slowing down. Half asleep, she checked the time and then hurried to the window. Peering from behind parted curtains, she thought she recognized the car. It was similar to the black sedan she had seen earlier and it was parked at the same spot. It was also just far enough away so that it was virtually impossible in the darkness to see anything other than its shape and that it was a dark color. Diane watched for almost ten minutes, hoping the driver might get out so that she could get a look at him. He didn't. The only other thing she could make out was a red glare as whoever it was dragged on a cigarette. She stood by the window long after the car was driven off, than went back to bed. It seemed as though she had barely fallen asleep when the phone rang.

"Oh, God," she muttered as she lifted the receiver. "You again."

"How's that?" the voice at the other end asked.

"Oh, nothing."

"Mrs. Duval?"

"Yes."

"This is Detective Joseph Spinaldo, Pittsburgh Police Department."

It took a few more seconds before she finally realized who was on the line. She looked at her wristwatch. Seven a.m.

"Wow, I must have finally slept soundly."

"Pardon me?"

It all came together. A policeman calling at seven a.m ... there had to be something wrong.

"My husband. You've found him."

There were a few moments of silence. "No, Mrs. Duval, not exactly, but his car has been located."

"But not my husband."

"No, ma'am."

"Where?"

"In a motel parking lot near Greensburg."

"Greensburg? What would he be doing there? That's sixty miles from Pittsburgh."

The policeman cleared his throat.

"No. Wait a minute," Diane exclaimed. "It can't be what you're thinking."

"Mrs. Duval, we have no idea what it is, or was, other than the car was there, in the parking lot."

"How'd they find it?"

"The motel manager. He said it had been parked there for three days. The police traced it by the license plate and of course, Bob Thomas did put out a stolen car bulletin marked 'urgent' after you came in."

"Where is it now?"

"At the police pound."

"Why? Why is it there and why are you involved?"

"Well, the people here want to check it out, and the case has been turned over to me."

"Then can I come down to pick it up?"

"I'm afraid not."

Diane could hear Spinaldo release a deep breath.

"Afraid not? Why not? And wait a minute. The case has been turned over to you. Why is there a case? You're a detective and it is now a case? That means something criminal has happened, isn't that right?"

"We're not sure when you can pick the car up, Mrs. Duval. They said they've found bloodstains and they want to find out how they got there. The forensic lab people asked me to ask you for your husband's blood type."

"Oh, God," she muttered. "The dream."

"The what?"

"Never mind, but bloodstains mean something's happened to him, don't they? And that's why you're on the case, I mean, when there's blood."

"It doesn't necessarily mean something has happened to him. But he is missing and there are stains. They want to find out if they are possibly his."

"Type O positive."

"You're sure?"

"Yes. It's on his Marine Corps dog tags. He showed them to me once. They're still around here someplace, but I am sure."

"Good."

"Now what do I do?"

"Nothing for now. Nothing you can do. Just sit tight and we'll call you. I'll be handling things from now on."

"A detective and not a regular policeman?"

"We're not so bad."

"I didn't mean it that way, but with a detective on the case, it's no longer a missing person status. It's more like a murder status, right?"

"We just want to do our best," Spinaldo assured her. "I've talked to the Greensburg police. A room was signed out in your husband's name and with his credit card. So, we know he was there, or at least someone was there with his identification and credit cards. I'm coming over a little later to pick up a photo of your husband. So if you can, get the most recent one you might have."

"He's dead, isn't he?"

"What makes you think that?"

"Well, what else is there to think?"

"It's no use thinking the worst. I'll be there in a little while, say, nine?"

Diane agreed to the time, and leaned back against a pillow after hanging up. It wasn't long afterward that she reached for the phone.

"Well, here comes step number two." She decided it was as good a time as any to call the families.

Each call lasted nearly a half hour. Both sets of parents were extremely upset. They had a lot of questions and weren't satisfied with many answers. They were most concerned about why she hadn't called earlier. That question was brought up several times until Diane finally lost her temper.

"What should I have done," she eventually asked both sets of parents, "called and said I think my husband is shacking up with another woman?"

It was an abrupt, even rude way of ending the conversations, but after nearly an hour of being berated from both sides of the family, Diane had had enough. She felt all four of them failed to consider her feelings and what she was going through. Nevertheless, she did admit that she probably should have let them know sooner and apologized. After declining her mother's offer to come over, she then assured both sets of parents that she'd call as soon as she heard anything. She breathed a deep sigh of relief after hanging up. She didn't tell them about the mysterious calls. There was still hope that Sergeant Thomas was right, and that it was the work of a prankster.

Eight o'clock and nothing to do but think again of all the possible things that could have happened to her husband or what he might have been involved in. Blood did not appear in a car without someone being shot, stabbed, beaten or in an accident.

She wished she had told Spinaldo to come at eight. She tried television again; she could watch it while making breakfast. As the set faded in, a scene that appeared in an early morning movie was of a gangster shootout. She didn't need that, and hurriedly switched channels until she found something less violent, cartoons. Nice, but a few scenes later, Elmer Fudd was firing a shotgun at Bugs Bunny.

"Bah!" She turned the TV off and went about her morning ritual, breakfast, and then a call to her employer informing him that she would still not be in. "Don't worry," he said. But the call was not without bothersome questions.

After that, she plopped back onto the sofa and thought about what might be next. She didn't have long to wait. She met Spinaldo at the door.

Chapter 8

The man smiled. Diane didn't. He moved toward the door. She gestured with her left hand in front of her to stop. Her other hand, holding a cocked Colt forty-five, was positioned behind the door.

"You're the detective?"

"Does that surprise you?" His smile accentuated near perfect teeth. "Joe Spinaldo."

He held his hand out to shake Diane's. By force of habit, she extended her right hand. The weapon was pointed directly at Spinaldo's mid-section.

"Whoa!" Spinaldo quickly stepped to one side as he saw that the weapon's hammer was in a firing position.

"You could have been anyone, and I was ready just in case."

"I guess you were. Now why don't you just point it away from me, uncock it put it aside?"

Diane didn't release the hammer. Instead, she stepped back. She still wasn't positive of the man's identity.

"Do you have any identification?"

During the few seconds it took Spinaldo to dig out his wallet and produce identification, Diane studied the man. He was nothing like she expected. Over the past week, she had met or seen policemen of all ages, shapes and forms. Like Sergeant Thomas, Spinaldo was completely different from the stereotype detective image: sport jacket, loose tie. Both resembled one of her husband's business colleagues, she thought. Spinaldo was tall, maybe a little over six feet. He had dark eyes, dark wavy hair and a small mustache. Skin a little dark; he was Italian, no doubt in her mind, and a very handsome one at that. A custom-tailored pin-stripe suit accentuated decently broad shoulders, and a body that appeared athletic but not overly muscular. Diane guessed his age to be the mid to late thirties.

He showed his badge and asked if he could come in. He was still worried about the cocked weapon.

Diane suddenly realized that she was staring and blocking the door, even after she checked Spinaldo's I.D. Embarrassed, she hurriedly stepped aside.

As Spinaldo entered, Marge Bennett followed him. She had been standing to one side, out of Diane's line of sight.

"Wait a minute." Diane said, blocking Bennett's entry. "What are you doing here? That's a hell of a sneaky way to get in here." She turned to Spinaldo for an explanation.

"She said she knew you."

"She does, in a way, but she's not welcome."

Spinaldo looked to Bennett and shrugged.

"I'm not going to interfere. Maybe I can help," Bennett said.

"I thought we settled that. Isn't that why this man is here?"

"Yes. I guess you're right. I'll go, but I'll still get part of the story here, and in Greensburg, and I can use my imagination for much of the rest. I really think it would be better for you that, when it does hit the papers, the facts are as accurate as possible."

"First of all, I don't see why it should even hit the papers, and secondly, what you're trying to do is blackmail or coerce me. But if it does appear in the papers, seldom have I ever read a newspaper story where all the facts were accurate. Most of them are via the reporter's imagination."

"Oh, come now, Mrs. Duval."

"Oh, come now, yourself, Miss Bennett. My father began a career as a reporter, so I'm not particularly dense on the subject. He always felt that a reporter's job was to report news from both sides, and then let the readers decide — just the facts, you know.

Editorializing was for the editors. But along comes a new breed — the yuppies — people like you, who under a guise of a thing they decided to call interpretive reporting, write anything, suggest anything, and conclude anything with no fear of retribution or regard for accuracy or honesty. Why? You don't have to reveal sources. Dad said that half the time the only sources are those conjured up by the writers themselves. That's why I don't want you here."

"Some of what you say might be true, but do you really think I'm the only reporter who goes to a police station? There are others. You know, we do have a couple papers in this town, and I can't say what others will write once they get wind of this. They have no idea about the car at this time. To them, even if they've given it any attention, it's still a husband who has taken off. But I already know that I can get times and dates, and therefore, I can write a decent story. And I don't know of any detective who covers run-of-the-mill missing husband complaints. I sure don't. It'd be a waste of time, but I just happened to stumble onto this by bumping into you a couple of times. And if you know journalism as you say you do, then you know it's my job to follow up.

"I can go back right now and write a story about your husband missing, his bloodstained car being found at a sleazy motel, and do a pretty good piece on it. I really didn't plan to write anything, at least not yet. I'd rather work with you and for you, but I still have a job to do, so you decide."

Bennett started toward the door, but wisely at a pace slow enough to give Diane time to consider what she said.

"Wait a minute." Diane turned toward Spinaldo. "I don't know what to do or think."

"It's up to you. She knew where I was going, and if she couldn't come with me, she'd just follow in her own car, and she'll still get a story out of it. I know her. She's been around. She's a good reporter, and if she says she wants to help, she wants to help. She's never interfered with any of my investigations, and none others that I know of."

"Stay."

Diane closed the door. She ushered them both to the living room, then took a few minutes to serve coffee, and apologized for not having breakfast rolls.

"This is fine," Spinaldo and Bennett said almost at the same time.

There was silence for a short time while they enjoyed the coffee.

"Good," Bennett raised the cup an inch or two.

Spinaldo agreed, and then began. "I guess by now you've surmised that we suspect some kind of foul play. As I mentioned there are bloodstains—pretty heavy—in the front passenger side. I'm presuming that your husband didn't carry a weapon or have one in the car."

Diane's hands were trembling to the point where her cup was rattling on the saucer. She set the cup on an end table and apologized.

"Don't worry. Relax. I'll wait."

"I'll be all right. I just don't go through this every day." She gave Spinaldo a weak smile, and then continued. "No, he never carried one, but as you saw, we do have a forty-five. It's licensed, but not for carrying. A friend, Jeff Felts, who is a police officer, works with us at a range. He's an expert marksman. I'm not Annie Oakley, but I can shoot."

"I know Jeff. He's a fine policeman," Spinaldo said. "Now, about the photo."

Diane nodded, went to the bedroom and returned with two prints. "These are the most recent, taken about a month ago."

"Any negatives?"

Diane sifted through the print envelope and handed Spinaldo the negatives. "What's the next step?"

"I'll go to Greensburg with this picture and see if the motel manager recognizes him."

"May I go with you?"

"You can, but are you sure you want to? It might be tough on you. We have to look toward the worst scenario and hope for the best. That could mean anything."

"I know what you're saying, but it's better than sitting around here, waiting and wondering. I've had enough of that."

Bennett turned toward Spinaldo. "Can I join you?"

"It's up to Mrs. Duval."

Bennett looked to Diane.

"I just don't want to be grilled."

"I'll leave that up to Joe."

Spinaldo turned to Diane. "I have some business downtown. It won't take long. Can you meet me at the station, say at three?"

"I'll be there."

Diane leaned her head against the door after they left, took a deep breath, and slowly released it. It was still like a bad dream.

Since she would be riding with Spinaldo, Diane decided to take a trolley to down town. She was just plain tired of driving and besides, it was always an interesting trip. No matter how many times she made it, there was always something she had never seen before. Right then, it helped to take her mind off her problem.

The squealing of metal wheels braking against iron rails snapped Diane out of her reverie. Spinaldo and Bennett were waiting at the base of the station steps. She didn't bother to explain why she rode the trolley, and they didn't ask. Spinaldo led the way to an unmarked car parked nearby, and it wasn't long before they were traveling east on the Penn-Lincoln Parkway.

There wasn't much conversation until Diane casually mentioned the experiences with the car and the phone calls. She did so merely to break the stillness and monotony. Nobody wanted to talk about the reason for the trip.

"Why the heck haven't you mentioned this stuff before?" Spinaldo asked.

"It was nothing. I'm sure the call was from a crank. Mr. Thomas thought so too. The car? Probably a friend of one of my neighbors."

"A strange car, nothing? A crank?" His slight chuckle was not one of delight. It was one of disbelief.

Diane wished that she wouldn't have brought up the subject.

Spinaldo shook his head.

"Why get so upset? I told Mr. Thomas. Didn't he tell you?"

"Why get so upset?" Spinaldo replied. After a few moments of silence, he continued. "No, he didn't tell me. I only had a few words with him. When was the last time you had a call like that? How many have you had?"

"A few, but I don't think ... "

"Well, you'd better start thinking,"

"Hey, back off." She turned to Bennett. "You've had those kind of calls, haven't you?"

"Sure, but not after somebody was missing. They were always more or less amusing. Someone always breathing heavy and whispering what he'd like to do with me. Sometimes it was fun listening. But Diane, this situation is different. Those guys were whack-offs. Whoever this is might be a whacko."

Spinaldo interrupted. "I'm sorry if I upset you, but this is deadly serious. No matter what, you must not hold anything back. I have to know everything; I mean everything. Your husband is missing and the caller might be the person responsible for that, most likely is. Did you ever stop to think, God forbid, that if he or anyone else has harmed your husband?"

"You mean has killed my husband," she interrupted.

"Whatever, but that someone has your address and your phone number. He or she has a key to your home and may be a psychopath. Also, that someone may just be the person puffing ciggy butts in the car you mentioned. You never saw that car in your neighborhood before, right?"

Diane nodded. She didn't answer, but the words sank in. She stared out the window.

Bennett's voice, as soft and as reassuring as could be, interrupted Diane's thoughts. "Diane, I think you'd better take Joe's advice. You could be in a great deal of danger."

"But I can't understand why you're getting involved. If I'm a target and you are involved, then you could also become a target."

"I know. You said your dad was a reporter. Then you ought to know this might be a huge story, or nothing. I try to ferret out stories. It appears, despite the car and the calls, to be no more than a meandering husband who eventually will come home. If that is the case, I forget it and get on with my business. But, we have this Greensburg situation and we have no idea where this will lead. I really hope it will be nothing. Regardless, I've covered stories where I could easily have been killed, but like I said, that's my business. I've been there before, and that's a chance I have to take. I'm always looking for something that will give me a break in this business. That's no different from your husband's desire to succeed at his business.

"I've been shot at, threatened by criminals I've written about, a passenger in a speeding police car when it crashed and turned over, and many other close calls. That comes with the territory, especially that of a good police beat reporter."

Diane didn't answer. She went back to staring at the passing countryside without really seeing it. Spinaldo or Bennett was unable to see the tears that trickled down her cheeks.

Chapter 8

Greensburg was small and attractive, like so many western Pennsylvania towns. At one time, it was a coal mining and railroad town, a stop on the way east. The roundhouse and depot were gone, diesel fuel finished off mining, and small businesses, manufacturers, and banking became its main activities.

Spinaldo drove through the downtown area twice. "I'm looking for a police car or the station." He anticipated their question before either woman could ask. He finally spotted a squad car and flagged it down. The car pulled up beside his so that both drivers faced each other. Spinaldo showed his identification and explained briefly why they were in town. He asked directions to the motel and then about its reputation.

"Yeah, I've heard about the car. Actually, it's about two miles east of town. Just follow this street. Worst place ever. Full of whores." He apologized to the women.

"Don't worry about it," Bennett said.

The policeman smiled and nodded.

"Two ways of looking at it, though. It's a headache, but at least we know where they are most of the time. I think the guy pays off somebody or it would have been closed down long ago. But then, they'd just migrate to somewhere else. Citizens complain about it now and then, but get nowhere and finally give up. At least until somebody else starts a new campaign. Pretty soon that also dies, and it's back to square one."

"Well, at least we aren't the only ones with problems like that," Spinaldo said after the policeman drove off. It was a few more moments before anyone spoke. Diane shook her head slowly, while biting her upper lip.

"God, I can't believe that Ron would be at a place like that. It's just not logical. Ron had no reason for a ..." She tried again. "He didn't have to depend on some —"

Bennett saved her, "Slow down Diane, your jumping to conclusions."

The World's End Motel was easy to find, a mile beyond the city limits. The layout was typical: two rows of rooms facing a center courtyard, an office at the entrance, abutted by a long-closed restaurant, its windows caked with a coat of dust and dirt. The courtyard was littered. A letter was missing from a flashing 'Vacancy' sign.

"This should be named the World's Pits Motel," Bennett said. "They probably never have to turn that sign off with the fast in and out clientele this place obviously caters to," she suggested. "Oh, God, me and my big mouth. I'm sorry."

Diane shook it off.

A man behind the desk looked up from a weekly trash magazine and smiled as they entered "Hey, a two bagger."

"That's enough." Spinaldo flipped open his wallet.

The owner held up his hands. "Sorry. Didn't mean anything personal."

Spinaldo showed the man a photo of Ron Duval.

"Has he been here recently?"

"Like how recently?"

"Like within the past week or two."

"No, but only as far as I know. Now, if he came with a you-know-who, then I probably wouldn't see him. The regular comes in before the fact and gets a key, then after the fact she pays up. Than everybody's gone. Or, he might have come when the other guy was on the desk."

"Okay, then. Take a look at your register, cards or whatever for a Ronald Duval."

Diane closed her eyes as the man flipped through a file card box.

He extracted a card.

"Oh, no," Diane whispered.

"Oh, yes. You his wife?"

"Never mind that," Spinaldo said.

The man placed the card on the counter so Spinaldo could read it.

"He did stay here for two nights, but that guy you showed me wasn't him. I remember him now. I checked him in. But this was a different guy."

"How different?"

"Big, dark long hair. Had a scar somewhere on his face, but I can't remember now just where. I really don't pay much attention to anyone, never do. We have regulars from the city, and I know better than to pay too much attention to anybody. This particular guy asked for a companion, so I lined him up. I remember him because he didn't look like a very nice person. Scared the s— ahh, scared the heck outta me."

After telling the man that a police artist would be visiting him in a day or so, Spinaldo turned to the women. "Well, that's it for here. There's nothing else we can do."

Not much was said on the way back to Pittsburgh and it wasn't until Spinaldo was approaching Pittsburgh proper that he spoke.

"Look, Mrs. Duval. Can I call you Diane?"

She nodded.

"Diane, I'm not going to pull punches. We've got a problem. If your husband wasn't with this guy, and I don't think he was, then this guy has done something to him. Whatever that is, we'll find out. But for now, you keep all of your windows and doors locked. As a matter of fact, have the locks changed right away. Don't open the door until you're positive who's on the other side. And use that same approach you used when I got there. Anyone calls or any cars start pulling up again, call me immediately."

He handed her a card. "I've jotted my home number on there also, so call. Okay?"

Diane nodded.

"I'll drive Mrs. Duval home," Bennett said.

The only sounds during much of the ride from the station were some deep sighs by Diane. She finally broke the silence. "I can't understand what Ron would be doing with a guy like that or with those kinds of women."

"I don't think your husband ever was at that motel. He may have been with the man for whatever reason, but I don't think he was with him when the guy signed in."

"Then what? Where could he be?"

"I wish I knew."

"Then if he wasn't there, that man isn't going to let him run around to sic the police on him, is he?"

Bennett was afraid to answer.

"You don't have to answer. He's dead. I know it. I wasn't born yesterday. He's dead. So maybe that was more than just a dream."

"I don't know."

"I do. I can't even begin to imagine that Ron would hand over his car, wallet and all of his credit cards to someone without a fight, and the bloodstains attest to that. He's dead."

"Maybe we're wrong. Maybe there's another answer. One thing for sure, there is something amiss. I hardly ever paid attention, as I said, to missing husbands. Wives, yes, sometimes, but from my experiences, husbands are usually out carousing around."

Minutes passed before Diane answered. "But this is different. We always had great sex, unless I really didn't know my own husband. Ron's dead. He wouldn't be doing this to me if he wasn't."

"Maybe he ditched everything. I mean, ran away from life itself, tossed his wallet and just disappeared, and this guy found it. Maybe everyday pressures got to him. That happens. I did a story once where a banker disappeared. He turned up two years later with another woman. It seemed everyday pressures did get to him, along with his wife, and he wanted away from it all. He was discovered when the police picked him up on a traffic violation. He was dumb enough to pick a small town to get lost in, and you don't pick a small town if you want to disappear. I think after a while, he wanted to be discovered."

"Than what?"

"Funny thing. They brought him home and thought there'd be a happy reunion, but his wife booted him out. She had hooked up with somebody else. Seems like her boyfriends were also among the pressures that got to him."

"And?"

"I don't know. It was no longer a story."

"So you think that could possibly be the case with us."

"No. Definitely not."

"The story really has no ending. You don't know what happened after that. But I am going to find the end to this story, and I'm serious when I say that. I don't have too much faith in police."

Bennett didn't answer.

"I mean, Joe Spinaldo is nice, but off to work he goes and we're supposed to just hold our breath."

"Do you think he can snap his fingers and solve the situation, or that this is all he has to pay attention to? You obviously don't know it, Diane, but some of those detectives have huge caseloads and some at this time have priority over yours. Up to the discovery of blood, I'm surprised that they gave it so much attention. You must have been convincing. But I guess no guy in his right mind would walk out on someone like you."

It wasn't long before Bennett turned onto Diane's street.

"Who knows," she said. "Maybe he's home right now, waiting."

"That's the same thing the cop said, and I've said that to myself every time I've been away," Diane murmured "It's just wishful thinking. Oh my God!"

"What?"

"Look. A light. There's a light on in the house."

"Maybe you left it on hurrying to get out."

"No. No, I didn't. I never leave a light on."

Bennett pulled into the driveway. Diane hurried out of the car and to the front door. She turned the handle and pushed, but there was no give. For a second, she looked quizzically, because once one of them got home, the door was never locked.

Bennett caught up and grabbed one of Diane's arms. "Good lord, Diane, stop!"

"For what? Can't you see he's home?"

"Then why is the door locked?"

"Who knows? We'll ask him."

"Diane, don't be stupid. Someone has your keys, and if it was your husband in there, don't you think the sound of the car and all this commotion would have brought him to the door?"

Diane's shoulders sagged. Then she perked up again. "Maybe he's hurt."

"If he made it home, then he could make it to the door. I think we should call Joe."

"What?"

"All right, then, just call out to your husband."

Diane stared at her.

"Yes, call him out loud so he can hear you."

Diane called. No answer. She knocked on the door, and then called loudly two more times, but still no answer. A few porch lights flicked on at neighboring homes. She looked back to Bennett.

"Diane, I don't think we should go in. I'm scared. Go next door and call Spinaldo. He's probably still at the station."

"No," Diane said, as she went to the car and returned with a huge knife. "Ron put this under my seat. He used to say, if a guy has a gun, it's all over anyway, but if he decides to reach in, then slice his arm. It's razor sharp. It was Ron's in the Marines. I think he called it a K-bar or something like that."

Diane unlocked the door and started in. Bennett followed.

"Leave this door open," she said. "If we have to run, I don't want to be bothered by having to open the damned thing."

"Ron?" Diane called in a subdued voice. There was no answer. They started toward the den where a light was on. She called a bit louder. There was still no answer. She turned to Bennett.

"Look carefully before we go in. Anyone could be hiding in there. I'm sweating down to my ass."

They stood perfectly still, listening for any sounds.

Diane turned to Bennett and whispered, "There's a note leaning against the desk lamp." They waited several more long moments before deciding that the room was empty.

"You go in. I'm staying by this door," Bennett said. "Is there another way out?"

"The door wall."

"Okay. If you hear this door slam, you'd better get that friggin' door wall open, but fast."

Diane nodded, and then hurried to the desk. "Oh God," she muttered. "Oh, no."

Bennett hurried in. Diane handed her the paper.

Pasted on the paper was a cutout from a pornographic magazine. It was of a naked man and woman fondling each other. A roughly drawn arrow pointed to the pubic area of the woman.

"You, my girl," was printed above the head of the woman. On the side of the photo was an arrow pointing to a scribbled-in oversized penis.

"Put it down, fast. Don't touch it anymore."

Diane looked puzzled.

"If there are prints on it, you don't want to mess them up," Bennett said. "Now you see what Spinaldo meant about some weirdo having keys to your home and also why I didn't want you dashing in here like some crazy fool. We'd better get the hell out of here right now."

Diane started toward the door.

"No!" Bennett restrained her. "He could be right outside the door just waiting for us to come busting out."

Bennett put a finger to her lips, tiptoed to the door wall, quietly slid it open, looked each way and slipped out. She motioned for Diane to follow. They sneaked around to the front. Nobody was in sight.

"God, I don't believe this," Diane said.

"Well, you'd better believe it. Somebody has plans for you, and judging from that bit of artwork, they ain't pretty. Call Joe right now."

Chapter 9

The arrival of a crime lab van, parked in front of Diane's house, assured Diane that the situation would no longer be kept quiet. It wasn't but a few minutes after the van arrived that Diane's next-door neighbor and others also arrived.

"What's going on, Diane?" Ruth Allen, her closest neighbor, asked.

"Nothing much."

"Nothing much? I don't remember ever seeing a police crime unit on this street. That's more than nothing much. Someone break in?"

The question deserved a simple "yes" answer and that would be it. Only it wasn't.

Another neighbor joined in. "What's wrong, Diane? Crime labs aren't called on ordinary break-ins. There was no crime lab when my house got ripped off. What's going on? Is Ron here?"

Spinaldo began to ask the people to go back to their homes, but Diane restrained him. *I might as well get it over with,* Diane decided. "No. Ron is missing. He's been missing for several days, and somebody broke into the house and left a note."

"Like a ransom note?"

Diane hated this, but it was bound to happen sooner of later. She knew her neighbors weren't trying to be wise or busybodies. She supposed she would have been curious and asking the same questions had this happened to one of them. If she was in their shoes, and a prowler, or worse, was in the neighborhood that could endanger her, she'd surly be asking questions. She took a deep breath and let it escape from puffed cheeks.

"It was a note with dirty pictures. And I don't know what's happened to Ron."

With gentle persuasion from Spinaldo, there were no more questions. The neighbors backed off, offered help if she needed any and quietly left. Diane thanked them and started for the house.

Diane stopped and faced Spinaldo. "Good lord, just a short time ago my life was as pleasant and quiet as could be. Not a worry in the world. Now..."

She had never seen a fingerprint person at work. The man dusted for prints throughout the house. He covered the doors, at least two feet above each handle.

"In case whoever it was pushed it. There could be a nice, full palm print," Spinaldo said as Diane looked on.

Then the man dusted the desk and lamps, and anything else he thought an intruder might have touched. He even went to the kitchen, and that surprised Diane. She followed. There was an empty glass on the counter.

"He might have been thirsty," the man said as he worked. Then he took her prints and asked her to show him something that her husband often handled. Diane led him to their bedroom, pointing out the alarm clock radio on his side of the bed.

The man took prints from the clock and then from the top dresser drawers. He answered before Diane could ask. The same question had been posed hundreds of times. "I'm taking them because they often get their jollies from touching or taking women's undergarments."

That's funny, she thought. Ron liked to touch hers and he wasn't a pervert. He just liked the feel of them against his skin, and she liked him doing it. It turned her on. Now the thought of someone else doing it was depressing. She followed Spinaldo to his car.

"I'll keep in close touch with you."

He held Diane's hand and gave it a slight squeeze.

During the following days, both parents visited, and they were awkward situations. Diane had told them of the calls and the car. Both couples assured her of their hope and care and extended offers to Diane to live with them where it might be safer. She turned them down. Spinaldo also suggested that she should move — maybe to her parent's home, but she turned his suggestion down, too. The possibilities were remote, she knew, but if Ron should return or even call, she wanted to be there.

Being there was more than difficult. There was no way possible that Diane could sleep for an entire night without being awakened again and again by noises that never before bothered her. She wished she could have barricaded the street. Every car that passed by, day and especially night, ignited a spark of hope, or despair. The mailman began to walk lightly past her house after Diane had hurriedly opened the door one day, thinking that the footsteps might be those of her husband.

She received another call. The man asked if she liked the picture he left on the table. Diane called Spinaldo right away. She asked if a tap could be put on her phone.

"It would be of no help," was Spinaldo's reply. "A guy like that may be crazy, but he's smart, too. He'd never call from a traceable number. He probably used pay phones from different locations. But I will ask my superiors if it can be done."

"Then if it can't be done, why am I calling you?"

"Because he might make a threat to get to you and we can set up some kind of trap. He'll make a mistake sooner or later, so you have to let us know about any calls. I have our people going through our files to pull out the name of every person who has had anything to do with a sex crime. But following up on all those people and where they are now all takes time."

"That's just great, but from the way he talks, time is something I don't have much of."

"I'm sure you do. Just hang in there. Have new locks put on your doors right away, and keep your windows locked. And finally, don't let any strangers in, even if they have some kind of utility uniform on. Simply, don't open the door for anyone, unless you know them personally."

Day or night, it was no longer a life but merely an existence. Nearly two weeks had passed since Ron disappeared, and surely if he were alive, he'd have been in touch by now. Diane had decided several days before the conversation with Spinaldo that she would have to adjust to a new life, if she lived long enough.

The first step was to get back to work. Her employers were lenient and helpful, but working proved difficult. By then, both papers had carried an article on her husband's disappearance and the discovery of the car. She was confronted each morning with the same questions: Any news? Have you heard anything? Any calls?

Her most trying experience every day was when she arrived home from work, shopping, or anywhere else, and had to case her own home. Each time she left the house, she left every light burning inside and out. She even had floodlights installed around the exterior. There'd be no chance of a dark corner when she arrived back home.

The ritual was the same every day. After setting any packages she was carrying on the front stoop, she navigated the house, checking for any sign of a forced entry. She would cock the forty-five and carry it carefully under a jacket or coat so the neighbors couldn't see it. They were jumpy enough, and she noticed that most of them now had all of their exterior lights on all night. Few neighbors ever greeted her. It was as though she were a leper. When her trek was completed, she then unlocked the front door as quietly as possible and peered into the living room. She kept the Colt at the ready, as Jeff Felts had taught her, when she checked rooms. It was exasperating, but she was not going to be caught off guard.

Soon, fewer questions at work were asked, and then none. Calls from Ron's colleagues ceased. Even her parents and in-laws, when they called or visited, other than asking if there was news, kept Ron's name and disappearance out of the conversations as much as possible. Their visits never lasted long. It was getting to a point where it was as though there might never had been a Ron Duval.

Than the black car was back again. She heard it just before daybreak. By than, she had accustomed herself to paying little attention to the scores of vehicles that passed the house every day unless any slowed down. When one did stop, day or night, she was at a window in seconds, with the Colt in hand.

She watched as the car pulled into the familiar spot: the short distance down the street shrouded in shadows. Someone in the car lit a cigarette as always, and its glow reflected in the side mirror each time the person drew on it. He knew what he was doing. He stayed only a few minutes, just long enough to torment her, and then drove off.

Diane knew even if she had a phone in her hand and called the police or Spinaldo, the car would be gone long before anyone arrived. The person was aware she was watching, she was sure, and she was also sure it was exactly what he wanted.

But she still called Spinaldo's home right away. No answer. She then called the station. As early as it was, she was told Spinaldo was out on an investigation. The policeman who answered the phone said he'd get the message to Spinaldo as quickly as possible.

What's the difference who answers? Diane thought as she hung up. *It's stupid to think that Spinaldo or anyone else on the Pittsburgh police force could or would do anything — not until there's a body, and when they do find a body, it will be mine and I won't give much of a damn then.*

Spinaldo's request for a tap be put on her phone was denied, even after he stressed more than likely that Ron Duval had been murdered and Diane was in dire danger. Should they tap the phone in every home where a husband or wife bugged out? His supervisor asked. The blood was common; it could have belonged to anyone, he was told. It wasn't as though they weren't convinced that somebody was threatening her and in some perverted way. But they also reminded Spinaldo of how many threatening calls during husband/wife feuds, or otherwise, they heard about every week.

Nobody had to tell Diane any more that it would take something a lot more threatening than a mysteriously parked car, a few calls and even a break-in to merit any kind of personal protection or wire tap. An attempt would have to be made on her life, at least, and that was not a pleasant thought. She told Spinaldo the police were like the Catholic hierarchy when it tried to justify someone for sainthood. They needed two eyewitnesses to a miracle. The police would probably demand that when an attempt on her life would be made, two persons better be watching.

"Why are the police so damned narrow minded?" Diane asked when Spinaldo told her a tap was nixed. "Maybe the man might just be stupid enough to call from a regular phone, especially if he made it from another city. If he's dumb enough, he could possible think that it couldn't be traced from that distance. Anything is worth trying. Unless someone drops Ron's body — or mine — in front of your captain's desk, this whole matter means little to anyone there."

"Anyone but me and my partner. It's not that my superiors don't really think that it could be more than a missing person, especially after the car was found, and the blood stains. But as dumb as it sounds, there are procedures that are followed, and this happens to have fallen in a gray area. He could have bled for any reason. He's missing. At this point, that's about all there is to it."

"So he's injured and he hurries to a sleazy, prostitute-infested motel for first aid. That sounds more like a deduction made by one of those idiot assistant detectives in Class B movies than real live detectives. I told Marge Bennett I didn't think the police knew what they were doing. I just might have been right."

Spinaldo didn't answer and as much as he hated to say it, "I'll be in touch" was the only way of ending an uncomfortable situation.

Diane forgot about wiretaps and caller I.D. Her mind was back to the present, on the car and its occupant. Whoever it was always made sure that Diane received a phone call within a short time after each visit. She had considered leaving the phone off the hook but she also received calls from others besides the man, so that was out of the question. Spinaldo could have some news, or maybe Ron might finally try to contact her.

Now she could see the advantage of having caller I.D. and decided to order it immediately. Until that was done, she couldn't avoid answering the phone, so she warmed up a cup of coffee, sat at the table and waited. She guessed he'd make it within ten minutes. She was close: thirteen. She didn't say a word after quietly lifting the receiver, hopeful that the caller might be Spinaldo answering her call.

"Diane?"

She recognized the voice, but still didn't speak. "Wait. Don't hang up. You hang up on me a lot." It was though he was pouting. "Don't you like me?" He paused for a few seconds. "Anyway, I hope you don't think I'd forget you just because you never want to talk. I didn't forget you when I left my artwork. I'm still hoping that you liked it."

"It was the work of a retarded pervert." Diane was finally remaining calm while talking to the man.

"I don't think so. I think it was pretty good."

"Only a low life mongrel like you would.'

He laughed.

"Why are you doing this to me? What did we ever do to you? What have you done to my husband?"

"Screw your husband. He's out of the picture." The man was shouting. "It's us now, you bitch. It's what we'll be doing when your time arrives."

"You've killed him."

"Did I say that?"

"Yes, just now."

He laughed again.

"You bastard."

Diane hung up the phone.

She returned to table and sipped her coffee. It was no longer hot, but she didn't mind. She rubbed an index finger around the rim of the cup as she contemplated again what the man meant by 'when your time arrives.'

Spinaldo called shortly after that and apologized for not being able to get to her earlier.

"Oddly enough, I was just about to call you, when our man here said you called me."

"Oh, sure you were," Diane answered with a sarcastic chuckle.

"Honestly. I was busy."

"I know. You had some big deal ten-cent shoplifting case that had to take precedence over a kidnapping and possible murder."

"Come on, now, Mrs. Duval," Spinaldo began.

Diane interrupted him. "Never mind."

Diane told Spinaldo about the conversation she had and that the man virtually admitted that he killed her husband. She also told him about the reference to a time when he'd see her.

Spinaldo informed her that there wasn't much anyone could do about the car or the call. Yet.

"I figured that."

"It doesn't mean that we're not doing anything, but this is a difficult situation. And like I said, he'll make a mistake, maybe when he decides to pay that visit, and we'll be waiting for him." Then he informed her that the blood from the car matched her husband's type and quickly assured her that it was so common it could have been anybody's.

"Wasn't that a foregone conclusion?" Diane said. "Whose blood would it be?"

Spinaldo didn't bother to answer the question. He continued.

"We want to try for a DNA match. That way we can be sure if it was his blood or someone else's. So we need another source like his toothbrush, something personal. Our men are looking for strands of hair in his car that might do the trick, but getting the correct hair might be a problem. I don't know much about how they do that."

"You won't have to bother. We have our own blood banked at Mercy Hospital. With the AIDS situation, we didn't want to chance blood off the shelf if we were ever in need."

"Great! We'll have a test done and I'll get back to you with the results as fast as we can."

"When's fast?"

"It might take a week or two."

"Week or two? That's great. You can dig me up at Calvary Cemetery and let me know the result."

"Well, it goes to the state police lab, and they've got things coming in from all over. I know it might seem like an unreasonable length of time, but we'll put an urgent on it."

"Doesn't everybody put an urgent on what they need done?"

"That's the problem. Everybody does. So we'll try to convince them that this really is extremely urgent."

"So while you and the state police are trying, I'll just hang around and wait to be kidnapped and murdered. Then the police can have a real time of it. Two missing, two murders and still no bodies."

"Look, Mrs. Duval, we're doing the best we can with what we have."

"That's interesting." Diane chuckled as she shook her head.

"What's that?"

"I've heard almost the same line from a couple other police people. I think it's something police are taught to say when they're in the police academy. Than it's graded on how convincing it is."

"You can think what you may, but we can't have a man standing out on your street or on your porch all day and night because you're getting phone calls and a parked car makes you nervous, even though your husband is missing. You know that's not what I think, but that's what the people here say. Even though I'd like to get there to check this guy out, we still can't arrest the man in the black car unless he has some incriminating evidence in his car. And we'd better be right if we do decide to search his car.

"I'm certain, if he is your man, he wouldn't be dumb enough to carry any weapons or any incriminating evidence when he does park. It's no crime to park and relax. The best our people can do is to suggest that he stays away. We have a shaky sketch of him and that's gone out all over the city — actually the state. And we do patrol your neighborhood more than usual. We just have to hope for a break."

Diane muttered a goodbye and placed the receiver gently into its cradle.

Chapter 10

It wasn't long after her conversation with Spinaldo that the phone rang again. Diane lifted the receiver but didn't speak, and when the other end was also silent, she hung up.

In a few seconds, it rang again.

"Hey, is anyone there?" she heard as soon as she lifted the receiver.

"Yes." Diane recognized Marge Bennett's voice. "Sorry, I just wasn't sure who was on your end. I'm still getting calls from my paramour. Had another a while ago."

"Did you call Spinaldo?"

"What else is new? He was nice as usual and had the same old story. They're working on it."

"Well, they still don't have much to work with."

"You sound just like Joe."

"I should. He told me that just a while ago. Must have been right after you guys talked. Anyway, are you gonna be home for a while?"

"So you haven't used up all your story possibilities?"

"Don't be so suspicious. Have you seen a story from me yet that hurt you? No, I'm not putting another story together — yet — but I do have a story that might be of real interest."

"What is it?"

"You gonna be home?"

"Yes."

"Then, I'm coming over."

"Okay, but announce yourself. I have weapons all over this place now. I'm bound and determined that if this nut shows up, I'm going to shoot him right in the — well, just announce yourself."

"You can bet you life — and — mine that I will. See you shortly."

An hour later, Bennett eyed the Colt forty-five as Diane ushered her in. She placed the weapon on a small table near the front door.

"I wasn't kidding. When I go to the kitchen, there's one on the table. I go to the bathroom, there's one on a stand next to the commode. And I know how to use them."

"You do?"

"Ron was an expert shot in the Marines. He helped me," Diane continued as she led the way to the kitchen. "We've spent a lot of time on the range with Jeff Felts, a police sergeant, a nice guy."

Diane motioned Bennett to a kitchen chair and poured coffee for both. "Fresh, just made it."

"I haven't talked to you for a while," Bennett said as she chose a chair. "How are you doing?"

Diane sat across from Bennett. "Terrible," she said. "I love Ron, and it just seems impossible that I may never see him again. I mean there should have been some last words — anything." She used a napkin to wipe away tears that she couldn't hold back. Her head drooped, and she ran an index finger slowly around the rim of her cup as she continued. "I've often read about how people felt when a loved one died, like they couldn't go on. But they were usually old, but never at our age. At least that's what I thought. And now he's gone and now I wonder if I'm going to make it. We had so many things planned."

She stopped for a few seconds and took a deep breath to regain her composure. "The man so much as told me that he killed Ron. I always hoped and prayed otherwise, but as everything stands, it is pretty much evident that Ron is dead."

Diane finished her coffee and poured refills for both. "Right now I'm reverting back to my childhood. When my parents went out for an evening, I'd balance a knife on the door handle so I'd hear if somebody was turning the knob. It was a good idea, but I would have been too scared to do anything about it. I hope that wouldn't be the case now."

"One doesn't often see a woman packing such a shooting iron," Bennett said. "I'm gonna have to call you Diane Oakley." They laughed.

"We're laughing, but I'm definitely serious, Marge. If that guy comes busting through that door, I'm not going to be caught defenseless. He'll have about five fast ones in him, and these are hollow heads. Ron said they'd tear a person's innards apart."

"Did Ron ever tell you they are illegal?"

"So what? Who cares? What he's doing is illegal. Fight fire with fire."

Diane told her how she had to inspect the complete house after every trip; then she told her about the latest call. "We know he has a key, but it's useless. Now he'd have to bust the door down. I had the locks changed and steel doors installed. Nothin' much else I can do."

Bennett nodded in agreement as she opened a small briefcase and extracted a copy of a news article. "I was reading *The Detroit News* last night. I'm from that area, about twenty miles west, so I always glance to see what's going on in murder city."

"Is it that bad?"

"It's bad enough so that every time they question one of the city department heads, he or she ends up doing a stretch. It's the only city in the world that I know of where the mayor — well a former mayor in this case — tosses a huge welcome home party for one of his convicted cronies when they get out of the clink. But it's in appreciation for that person having taken a rap for him. Believe it or not, a former police chief is doing a long stretch for criminal activities. The police chief!"

"Wasn't it Al Capone who said eighty percent of the cops in Chicago were on his payroll?"

"Right. And Daly, when he was mayor of Chicago, had nothing on the establishment in Detroit. But let's forget that."

Bennett spread the article in front of Diane. "Take a look at this."

Diane read the headline out loud. "Wife of Missing Husband Found Murdered. That's too bad, but what's that got to do with me?" Diane pushed the article back toward Bennett. She didn't bother to read beyond the headline.

"I'll tell you what I think it has to do with you. And you would have seen it too if you had read on. This is exactly the same situation in which you find yourself. This woman's husband disappeared. Family members and police said she received mysterious phone calls for weeks. But they were considered merely to be crank calls — just like the cops here, other than Joe, are doing with you. They couldn't do anything. Doesn't that sound familiar? So the woman ends up raped, mutilated and murdered.

"If you would have read further, you would have also found that it didn't say much about how severely she was mutilated. But I called a friend of mine who works for *The Detroit News*. She checked and said that the woman was actually tortured, raped and then cut up pretty badly. Whoever did it removed her breasts and then used the knife... Well, never mind that, but I think you get the picture."

"And you think that's in my future?"

"Doesn't it sound like it?"

"Any gruesome murder would sound like it. I wonder how many persons are murdered like that. I find it difficult to believe there might be a connection, especially in a city some three or four hundred miles away."

Diane continued fingering the article and pulled it back toward her again, but did not read it. She waved it a bit as she continued.

"Here's what I think. I think somebody knows that my husband is gone, maybe even a cop, and he calls. He masturbates while I'm on the line and he's fantasizing, and that's it."

"Sure, and if you believe that, then why are you worried and why is your husband missing — dead as you now suspect? You're right, Diane. That does happen a lot. But don't forget, this character called you before most anyone else knew about Ron's disappearance."

Diane shrugged. Bennett continued. "I think we should really check this Detroit thing out. It's only a five or six-hour drive and I'll foot the bill. What do you say?"

"I don't think so. What about the police? Can't they do something?"

"Well, how long have you been waiting for the police to do something? Maybe we can persuade them if we can tie these things together. I already mentioned it to Joe, thinking he might want to go with us or us with him. Got the usual, 'We'll look into that' answer along with a thanks."

"I don't know, especially if Joe Spinaldo didn't get too excited about it."

"Well, I'm excited. What if there is?"

Diane shrugged again.

Bennett returned the gesture. "Won't your shoulders get tired from all this shrugging? The only thing it can possibly waste is a day. On the other hand, if there is a connection, it could help save your life and maybe a hell of a lot of pain and suffering to boot."

"You really think it's worthwhile?"

"Would I have come busting over here when I know you don't want people bothering you, especially me?" Bennett nodded toward the weapon. "How long do you want to have to lug those things around?"

"When?"

"I'll pick you up tomorrow bright and early, say around six."

"I'll be ready. I'll have to call my boss while on the way. But again, I'm still wondering why you're so wrapped up in this."

"I'm not pulling your leg or a fast one just for a story. Like before, I'm telling you I believe this is super serious. Certainly, there could be tremendous news potential in it, and I am a reporter. Also, I don't think you or any other woman, me, for instance, should be put through something like this. So I'd also like to see the bastard put down. Does that make sense?"

"As long as he doesn't put us down."

Diane slept halfway through Ohio. It was the first time in days that she could sleep without being awakened by the sound of a car or the ringing of her phone. The rest of the trip was spent in idle conversation, during which time they exchanged backgrounds. They were surprised to find that they had much in common.

Both attended the University of Pittsburgh at the same time, but in different major areas, so they never met. Bennett majored in Journalism and went from college to a daily in Greenville, a small western Pennsylvania town.

"It was a good starting experience, but I didn't like it. I wanted more freedom to write features and columns and reviews. The editor, an older fellow, had me doing nothing but obits, rewrites and boring calls to hospitals, funeral homes and such. Later, *The Youngstown Vindicator Newspaper* hired me. Youngstown was a hell of a city — big time rackets, bombings, Mafioso-type gangs trying to muscle in on each other's turfs.

"That's when I really became interested in crime and its impact on a city. Years before I got there, Youngstown was referred to as the bomb capital of the country, before bombing became the vogue. When I interviewed for *The Pittsburgh Press*, there happened to be a police beat job open, and the Youngstown experience helped me cinch that job.

"Like I told you, I've been shot at, held hostage, hugged the ground during a shootout with bullets whizzing over my head and that crash going seventy miles an hour or more. But it sure'n hell beat the obits and stuff."

"That sounds like a hell of a lot of fun, just the kind of job every young girl would love to have."

"Well, Miss Funny Ass, you'd be surprised how many really would like this job, including you. I'll tell you, it's not as boring as all-hell nine to five jobs."

"I guess not. That's the kind of job I have. Who shot at you?"

"Sometimes the police let me tag along on a run if they thought it wasn't going to be dangerous. One went haywire and they ran into a drug situation. I was assumed to be a woman narc. I heard the bullet whiz right past by my ear, and the thud as it lodged into a utility pole a few inches away."

Bennett reached down the front of her blouse and pulled out a necklace. A flattened slug was attached.

"Here it is. I wear it for good luck. Had it on the night we flipped over. Didn't get a scratch."

"Anyone else get hurt?"

"Driver got a broken arm. The other cop had two broken ribs. Guess we all were lucky."

"Were you ever married?" Diane asked.

"I was too busy to get married. I went with a couple guys. Then I met Georgie, but he turned out to be gay. Hung around with another guy for a short time. He didn't like my being on a police beat and always sticking my nose where there was trouble. He thought I should have been home, cooking."

Bennett tossed her head back slightly and laughed. "The jackass said my life style wasn't compatible with his profession. Can you imagine a guy saying that to a woman, like my job wasn't compatible with his?"

"He was a pharmacist, a boring job if ever there was one, at least to me, and he was envious. People at parties and such were always asking me about things I was into. Nobody ever asked what kind of pills he was mixing. Except for my four-year stint, nobody else has come around that interested me enough. Now, Joe Spinaldo — there's a guy who could change things real fast for me."

After a few moments, Bennett continued. "How about you? Was Ron your first?"

"No, I had a couple beaus before him. I actually was going with another guy when we met. I didn't like Ron at first. I always heard that from others, that they didn't like their husbands when they first met. That was the case with me. Then we dated a couple times and things picked up from there. We got married in our junior year. It was fun, school, no work, just play. I thought we had a pretty nice life afterwards. Both working; both with decent jobs. Buying a home. We were thinking about adopting some kids. And now, this."

There was a lull in the conversation. It was the first time Diane had been to western Ohio in a car. She knew right away that she would never like living there. The land was flat, no hills. No real landscape.

"Dreary. What do they do for winter fun, like sledding, in a place like this?" she asked, as they drove through the outskirts of Toledo. "There's not a hill in sight."

"They do have a couple man-made hills where I come from, where the kids can sled ride, and then there are some knolls in some of the parks." Bennett answered. "I used to have fun on them. When that's all there is, you assume that's all there is."

"Knolls?" Diane scoffed. "That would be a waste of time. Our sled runs were steep and like a quarter of a mile long. You could really fly. The city would close off a couple blocks for us, then spread sand or ashes at the end of the run so we wouldn't run into traffic."

"You don't have to prove that to me. I've been driving Pennsylvania hills for years now. After I moved to Pennsylvania, I realized there wasn't a hill where I grew up worth worrying about. Hines Park had a hill they called Dead Man's Hill. It was supposed to be dangerous, but it wasn't even close to being as steep as some of the everyday sled runs I see in Pittsburgh."

After a few minutes of silence, Diane asked Bennett if she had ever been involved in a situation where a woman was attacked, mutilated, and then murdered.

"Not all three."

"I always wondered what went through a victim's mind during the time she was being put through such an ordeal." Diane said. "Are many solved?"

"Sometimes by luck, when a woman escapes or someone sees it going down and gets a license number. But it's almost like the old Sherlock Holmes bit: the perpetrator always returns to the scene of the crime. Sooner or later, they do. Maybe out of morbid curiosity, like an arsonist who turns in the alarm and then helps to put out the fire.

"There was a case in Chicago a while back where this guy was murdering women. Then, one time he acted as though he discovered a body and led the police to it. It turned out that he was the killer, and had murdered seven other women. They thought maybe he wanted to get caught. I didn't. He thought trying to outfox the police was a rush, but he made a mistake along the way."

"Marge, if you're right, I wonder what this guy is like."

"From what my friend said, he'd be classified as extremely bad, a real psycho."

Diane's first view of Detroit's suburbs was as disappointing as those she had in Ohio. Later, as they drove through the downtown riverfront section, she found it bustling and modern. It was vastly different beyond that part of the city. The sections they drove through were disasters. They passed blocks at a time where most buildings were boarded up and debris cluttered sidewalks.

They traveled Woodward Avenue, formerly one of Detroit's busiest and most attractive shopping thoroughfares. It was desolate. A huge, seven-story building had to have housed something important. It was boarded up, decaying.

"That was Hudson's Department Store," Bennett said, "as nice as any in the country, a fantastic place just to meander through. Seven stories of it."

"What happened?"

"What happened?" Bennett answered with a chuckle and a slight shake of her head. "What happened to this whole place?" She waved from left to right across the steering wheel. "People are what happened. First of all, the stores were shoplifted to death, Hudson's included. Since most of the perpetrators were minorities, and nobody in upper levels of government wanted to admit it or do anything about it, the stores packed it in and moved to the suburbs. And there was, and still is, a lot of crime. Many of the smaller stores also moved out and nobody moved in. Because of the high rate of crime, people by the thousands fled the city. City officials, along with gullible media people, had to blame it on somebody, so they called it 'white flight' because a lot of white families moved out due to the crime. But there was black flight, too, when thousands of minorities fled Detroit. However, that fact was never mentioned by the media, at least when I was there.

"I remember the great toy lands at Hudson's. It's too bad for kids now, because malls have nothing other than bright lights. There are shops by the river in Detroit, but they're small and expensive and cater strictly to the upper crust. There's little downtown for the plain folks."

"What about the police?"

"One time I got ripped off at one of the festivals in a place called Hart Plaza, a huge waterfront park area. The policemen I intercepted asked me where I was from. Garden City, I told them. One stuck his face close to mine and snarled, 'Then get the hell back to Garden City and stay there.'"

"That's hard to believe."

"Well, believe it. That's Detroit."

Shortly afterward, they parked in an underground garage just off the riverfront.

"I called my friend before we left. She'll meet us for lunch in Greek Town. That's one of the few decent areas remaining in downtown Detroit. We'll get there by a people mover, which by the way is another money-losing fiasco. Runs millions in the red every year."

Greek Town was bustling. There were no boarded-up structures. Buildings housed cafes, restaurants, delis or ice cream parlors and it was evident that people had little fear of crime.

"This part is still very nice, only because business people decided to do something about it and put tons of pressure on city hall. But that would be impossible for the whole city. Besides, the city government had been so corrupt over the past twenty years that it wouldn't let many businesses dictate."

"And sometimes I thought Pittsburgh was bad," Diane said.

"No, it isn't. When Pittsburgh's steel mills closed down, most thought the city would die. Those in office may not have been perfect, but they didn't quit, or maybe didn't let crooks take over city hall. That's the difference."

They parked in a lot on Beubian Street where Bennett took Diane by an arm and guided her toward The Pegasus, one of the many Greek restaurants.

Chapter 11

The restaurant wasn't at all what Diane had expected. When Bennett talked about a Greek restaurant, Diane expected gothic type decor, maybe special artwork depicting scenes from Greece. She remembered the Brass Rail restaurant in downtown Pittsburgh, with huge pictures on every wall depicting scenes of waterways and ancient ruins and such. As a child, she read all kinds of things into those pictures. The Pegasus was no different from any ordinary restaurant: a counter by the front door, two separate dining rooms, booths in the front, tables in the rear.

"What's so special about this place?"

"Good Greek food. Other than that, it's not anything special, but you'd be surprised at how many Detroiters and visitors eat here."

A waiter intercepted them. "Is your name Marge Bennett?"

Not even a Greek accent, Diane said to herself.

They followed the waiter.

"See what I mean? Highbrows."

"Oh, yeah. We're highbrows, all right. Just ask Pittsburgh's police how highbrow I am. They have a hard time even talking to me."

"She beat us to it." Marge smiled and waved to a woman in a booth across the room. They exchanged hugs and Marge introduced Diane. "This is Audrey Pepper, a long-time friend of mine. We date back to our sorority."

"Come on. It wasn't that long ago. You make us sound like some old biddies at a reunion."

"You're right, but we are getting there."

Diane waved slightly as she slid into the booth. "Hey, wait a minute. I went to Pitt at the same time as you guys."

"Sorry, I should have said present company excluded. I hope you don't mind, I ordered for us already." She looked to Diane.

"You'll love the special veal plate they serve here and the Greek salad."

Diane smiled, although she would have liked to order her own food. She hated other people ordering for her. What if she didn't like the dish? Then she'd have to force-feed herself, come close to throwing up and yet smile and say, "Oh that was delicious."

Marge motioned to a waiter and ordered a round of beer. Bennett and Pepper complimented each other on everything from looks to clothes. They talked about what they were doing on the newspapers, and some of the things that happened to each since last they were together. Then the subject turned to boyfriends.

Boyfriends, sloyfriends, jobs, assignments, so what? Diane thought. She had lost interest early in their conversation. She resented having to sit like a dummy and smile every now and then, as though she were enjoying their recollections. She remembered how many times she and friends had put others through the same agony.

She was in a hurry to get on with the business they came for, anxious to see what was in a large manila envelope tucked under Pepper's purse. However, time didn't make much difference right then. They weren't going anywhere. Even though she tried to mask her discomfort, Marge finally noticed it.

"What about it?" Bennett motioned toward the envelope. "You have some stuff for us, right?"

"Oh, yeah, do I ever. Lots. I have a few friends on the force. They smuggled this file to me. Actually, even though a lot of time as elapsed, the case is still open, so if I lose it, I lose my ass, too. Or

I might have to give it to one of them. This stuff is definitely not pretty. As a matter of fact, it's downright ugly. I had a hell of a time looking at some of it. Could hardly finish or believe. It's gory, really bad stuff."

"So?" Diane said. "Do you think I came all the way from Pittsburgh not to find out what happened to this woman? We both want to know."

She nodded toward Bennett. "Marge here seems to think that someone might have the same plan for me." A light chuckle proved to be a feeble attempt to disguise the fact that she was nervous and well aware that Pepper's fear was legitimate. "It isn't often that one is forewarned about how he or she will die."

Pepper looked to Bennett and subtly pointed toward Diane, with an index finger moving back and forth, not more than an inch above the table. "This is..."

"Yes. Diane is the person I told you about. I thought you understood that."

"Oh, my," Pepper whispered. "No, I didn't. I thought she was one of your colleagues who was working on the situation with you."

"Well, we are sort of working on it together. We met shortly after her husband disappeared."

Pepper released a deep breath. "Maybe it's just as well that I did come on so strong. Honestly, it might be best not talk about it right now or look at the photos, especially if you think this kind of thing might possibly be in store for you." She shook her head slowly to emphasize the point.

"First of all, I do want to know, since I've come all this way, and secondly, perhaps you're being a little melodramatic," Diane said with a strained smile. "You're not writing a story now. It can't be that bad."

Bennett interrupted, sure that Pepper knew what she was talking about. "Since Diane and I need to know, maybe you can tell us a little before we go to the envelope. Perhaps we won't even have to bother with its contents."

Bennett was aware what the photos might look like, and thought she could spare Diane the shock and grief. It was a feeble attempt.

The waitress arrived just then with their orders. They ate mostly in silence. Whatever conversation pertained mostly to Diane's background. The last bites were hardly taken before Diane suggested they get on with the business at hand.

Pepper clutched the envelope close to her chest, looked directly to Diane, and hesitated almost between each word. "You said it can't be that bad. Well, I'm telling you, it is. These photos almost made me sick, and I've seen some bad scenes."

"I've heard that a couple times already, but isn't that what we came for?" Diane looked to Bennett for support.

Bennett reluctantly but silently agreed with a nod.

Pepper hesitated for a few seconds before deciding where to begin. "There was a history of calls, obscene. At least, that's what the police were told. And according to their reports, the calls started right after her husband disappeared."

"Just like Diane's," Bennett interjected.

Pepper looked at Diane for a few seconds, then continued. "The officer in charge said the woman even thought for a while that it might be her husband, disguising his voice, because some of the things the caller said could only have been known by her husband.

"But the police sort of discounted that. They felt a lot of people do and say a lot of the same things during sex. They suggested the guy guessed right on a couple of them, and she assumed that it was her husband. After another call or two, she realized it wasn't and became more worried and than panicky as the calls turned into threats of violence, promises of death, and more graphic and frequent."

"What did the police do?" Diane asked.

"What could they do? Nothing. They were crank calls, at least up until the time they found his car. It was abandoned in a red light district."

Diane looked quickly to Bennett.

"Yeah," Bennett said, raising an eyebrow. "Sounds familiar, doesn't it?"

"What?" Pepper asked.

"It's exactly what's happening with Diane." Bennett described the calls and where Ron's car was found.

"Wow, that is interesting," Pepper said. "In the situation here, the police figured that her husband decided to bug out. They suggested he just left the car after getting what he went there for, then said to hell with everything and took a powder. Plane, train, who knows? The couple did have some marital problems."

"But we didn't," Diane quickly interjected.

"Marriage problems are usually by degree," Bennett said. "You might consider one of yours as minor, while someone else might consider it as major. All depends on personalities and a few other factors." She turned back to Pepper. "And the calls?"

"Didn't pay too much attention. Like I said, they always considered them as crank calls. The story was carried in *The Free Press* and *The Detroit News* for a day or two about the husband mysteriously missing. Than it died."

"Actually, the police decided there really wasn't a crime in the red light district or elsewhere, so they put his absence on the back burner, a husband on the lam, pressing demands and all that stuff.

"So, one day some hunters' dogs sniff and dig into a shallow grave way out in the boonies, guess what they found? So the police get on it because — boy oh boy — now there's a body. The widow thought there might not have been a body if the police had taken her seriously. Then it was her turn."

"That's what those idiots in Pittsburgh are doing, waiting for me to get my ass taken apart," Diane said. "I'll finally get murdered, and then they can do something for me by investigating my death."

"I doubt if the police could have saved his life or Ron's, for that matter, if they would have started on the case immediately," Bennett stressed. "There was no reason, with what it seemed like at first, an every day missing husband, that they should have become suspicious," Bennett stressed. "Again, it's so much like

Diane's situation. We think Diane's husband was killed right away, or at least shortly after his abduction, and that was probably the case here. But how could anyone suspect that it was anything more than the usual stray, other than the wife?"

"That's easy to understand," Pepper said. "Well, anyhow, the police are still, to this day, stymied. There were no clues — nothing."

Pepper took a long sip of beer and resumed. "You sure you want to continue? Isn't knowing what happened enough?"

"No, it isn't."

Diane knew being told what had happened was really sufficient, but by then curiosity — no doubt morbid — captured her interest. Besides, if a gruesome death really was planned for her, she wanted to be made well aware. She could handle it, she was sure.

"It might make you sick."

Diane scoffed.

"Okay," Pepper whispered, as she removed the first photo, laying it face down on the table. She pushed it slowly toward Diane.

Diane turned it over. She was taken completely by surprise, even after having been warned. She closed her eyes, tilted her head back and slowly looked toward the photo again. She bit her lip, feeling the color drain from her face. "Oh, God," she muttered,

"I warned you."

"You're right. I just can't believe it's for real."

No one spoke. Diane stared at the photo. It was in color, which made it all the more vivid. A close-up from the top of the head on a slight angle showed the woman's body dangling over the side of the bed. She was on her back — nude. Her head was nearly severed, dangling by a mere slip of skin. Her hair was matted with blood. Her eyes stared. Her mouth was wide open with what might have been a final scream that never escaped.

Diane leaned back heavily against the booth. She tried to swallow, but it was nearly impossible. The beer she had sipped was at the top of her throat, threatening to come up all the way. She fought it back, telling herself she could not throw up, not after assuring Pepper that she could handle things. She finally regained a semblance of composure and pushed the photo back across the table. Pepper slipped the remaining photos back into the envelope.

"No," Diane whispered, stopping Pepper with a hand. "Go on."

"Go on? Are you sure?"

"Yes."

The second photo was taken from a different angle, showing the wall behind the woman. There were obscene words and sketches written and drawn with the woman's blood.

"Good lord," Bennett whispered. "He's used her body and blood as an inkwell. That poor woman."

"Oh, shit."

Diane felt herself going limp. She was wet and clammy, like after she exercised or ran. But she was determined to continue. She had to. It was ghastly, but she knew she wouldn't be satisfied until she saw or knew everything that had been done to the woman.

Diane had seen lots of blood, guts and gore in movies and television. Blood all over the place, but it was always pretend, almost amusing to watch. It was something absurd, something that could never happen to those degrees in real life. The bloody scenes, products of some scriptwriter's imagination, were made realistic by special effects expertise. Exploding bodies, heads toppling off torsos, bloody faces with eyes staring blankly out to the audience. After the initial shock, the sequences often resulted in giggling and sometimes outright laughter, and Diane was guilty of both at times.

She was now seeing one of those seemingly absurd scenes from a new perspective. No imagination, it was real: a person, once alive, subjected to treatment far worse than any writer had ever concocted. More sickening than any film she'd ever seen. More frightening yet was the thought that somebody might be planning to do the same to her. Pepper began putting other photos back into the envelope. Diane restrained her.

"Go on."

"Don't look at any more," Pepper pleaded. "Why? You've seen enough."

"She's right," Bennett added.

"Maybe she's wrong. I came to find out what someone might have in store for me. Knowing will give me the strength or the will to thwart him if, in fact, this is really connected to what I've been subjected to."

Diane wondered why she had to continue. She knew she'd seen enough. What she said didn't make sense and she knew it. She realized that it was morbid curiosity, like her teenage trip to the morgue. She had to go on.

"I still wish you wouldn't," Pepper said as she extracted the next photo and placed it face down in front of Diane.

Diane paid no attention and turned the photo over. She began to tremble. Bennett took her by the arm, even though she, too, was shaking.

"I'm all right. At least I think I am. But this is impossible to believe."

The photo was taken from the feet first. The woman's body was sliced from her crotch, upward over her abdomen and between what had been her breasts. The weapon, a large butcher knife, was plunged deeply into her chest.

"The coroner's report indicated she might have still been alive when he started that on her," Pepper said quietly. "Can you imagine what that person had to have gone through?"

Diane mumbled something, more moans than words. She was unable to hold back tears. Her trembling worsened. She pushed the photo back across the table. She'd had enough. Unable to speak, she leaned back and kept shaking her head. Her throat shut down. She couldn't swallow. She could barely breathe. She tried desperately to hold it back, but everything she ate came up. She cried, embarrassed and dizzy. She tried to apologize. Her lips moved, but there were no words. Tears streamed down her cheeks. She tried to find Bennett for support. But everything in the room began to spin, and then Diane lost consciousness. "God, oh

God," she was muttering when she came to. She became aware of hazy figures hovering over her."

"Relax, Diane. Just relax."

She recognized Bennett's voice. It was almost as though the words were drawn out, low pitched and echoing from far away. She slowly regained her senses. Her head felt as though it was tied to a weight and she gave up trying to lift it. Things slowly began to come into focus. Pepper's blurred face became clear. Then she saw Bennett at her side, dipping a towel into a pan of ice water. Others, whom she didn't know, were crowded around. A bus boy was already cleaning up her vomit.

"What happened?"

Her choked and burning throat barely released the words. There was a terrible, bitter taste in her mouth.

"You fainted," someone said.

Five minutes passed before Diane completely regained her senses. Sobbing, she apologized over and over during that time.

"Come on," Pepper offered. "No need for that. It was tough to take, but I warned you."

Diane managed a sickly smile. "Oh my God, he's planning that for me."

"Wait a minute," Bennett stopped her. "We don't know that for sure. This may be just what you thought before, nothing more than a coincidence. I mean, everybody who gets obscene calls could feel that way if they saw those pictures."

"Oh, yes, but does everybody have a husband who turns up missing and probably murdered?" Bennett was about to answer, but Diane stopped her. "Please, Marge. I know you're trying to make it easier for me. But don't. If this is really connected, I'll be damned if I'm going to ever let this son of a bitch do that to me. If I can't do anything more, I'll kill myself first."

Bennett couldn't help smiling as she looked at the few persons still nearby, trying to make sense out of the conversation.

By then, two bus boys helped Diane into a sitting position in the booth. Bennett wiped the perspiration from her brow.

"God, that feels good."

"You okay now?"

"I think so."

"Good," Bennett said. She handed her a glass of iced water. "Now drink this, and I have a sneaky notion they'd like to see us leave."

Chapter 12

Few words were spoken during the first fifty or so miles of the return trip to Pittsburgh, other than comments here and there about traffic or sights. Finally, Diane looked toward Bennett, took a deep breath, and broached the subject they both had been thinking about since they left Detroit.

"What do you think?"

Bennett also took a deep breath and let it escape slowly through puffed cheeks. "I don't know. I've been meditating it since we left. I guess we both have. I keep asking myself if this is just a weird coincidence or if this guy really is the same person who's been on your case. I keep coming up with the same answer. Yes, he is one and the same. And as absurd as it might sound, I'm thinking that he's on some kind of insane schedule, since he has said a couple times something about your time not being up yet. To me, it doesn't seem like some helter skelter thing where someone just goes around haphazardly doing women in. I'd bet he's done this in more than one city, maybe a lot, and if so, where? That's what we've got to find out, and then maybe we can piece some things together."

Bennett waited for a few minutes before continuing. "And those photos... it's hard to believe. I've covered some serial killer instances and was at a hospital when one a victim died, and I know how ugly things can get. This is worse than any of them."

"This puzzle, where would we start?"

"I've been thinking about that, too, since we left. There are sources that both of us can check into. If we find that our suspicions are well founded, then we'll get back with Joe Spinaldo."

"So, you're pretty sure that the Detroit situation and mine are the work of the same person?"

"What do you think I've been saying? Yes, I think they definitely are. And here's the way this Detroit thing might have gone down. She gets calls like you get. The police, just like your case, assure her that it's just some crank, and he'll eventually get tired of calling and stop. If nobody finds her husband, the police will continue to classify it as a husband who probably decided to bug out, and continue to tell her that the calls will soon stop. But the calls don't stop. They become more vulgar and threatening, but old faithful still believes what the police said. What else could she do but hope, like you, while you thought Ron might be alive? Now, the car is found in some sleazy area and before anyone can put anything together, bang! The woman gets it.

"The police then get busy trying to track a murderer. But the catch is, he's smart. He knows, probably from experience, that the police will think it's someone local, maybe even the husband. And while they are looking to and fro for him, the murderer is pestering you, or in some other city doing the same thing to another woman. The mitigating factor here is that we accidentally met and I happened to come across the story, and slowly, but maybe surely, we're starting to find things out. Those photos back there told us as loud as a boom box, we'd better be super careful."

"You're scaring the hell out of me, but I still say I will not get caught by surprise."

"You mean you think you won't. But what if my schedule theory is wrong and this man doesn't bother you for another month or even a year and by that time you've decided it really was a crank? Then, one day someone is at your door. Unsuspecting Diane opens it, and there he is, in broad daylight, bigger than life, and dressed up like a meter reader or something that nobody, not even yourself, would suspect. Then what?"

"You should be a script writer."

"Like hell. I don't write fiction. I think, calculate and write cold, hard facts, and what we saw back in Detroit was no Saturday night movie special. They were cold, hard facts. I'm scared. I'll tell you, that if this is the same person, then he is out to get you sooner or later for fun and games — his kind, not yours. That's my theory, and that's why we are going to do some research, and fast."

"What about Joe?"

"What about him?"

"Don't you think he could have figured out the same thing?"

"Possibly, but he doesn't know what we know, and how many of these missing person cases do you think there are? Scads. Has anybody, including us, presented him with this theory in detail? We will. I just told him we were going to Detroit to follow up on some possibilities. I don't think he's dragging his feet. I know he's concerned. But we've got one incident to think about. He's got a drawer full. He'll help. I'll guarantee you that."

"What makes you think so?"

"Someone like you hanging onto him for help. He'd be crazy not to. He's probably already got the hots for you."

"God, you have stupid ideas. That's ridiculous. You know I'm still married."

After she said that, she hurriedly looked away from Bennett, toward the outside mirror.

"Is it stupid? Don't kid yourself. And I'll bet anything that if you'd be truthful, you've given him some thought."

"Don't be ridiculous. He's nice and good-looking and that's all."

They drove for a while in silence, and then Bennett giggled.

"What?"

"Isn't it exhilarating, too, to think that we might possibly have one up on Pittsburgh's finest, and maybe solve a long string of nation-wide serial murders?"

"Oh, yeah. You do have pipe dreams, so when you come down out of the clouds, let me know where we start this research."

"For you, it's a library."

"Library?"

"Yes. You're going to spend a lot of time at Carnegie Library there on Forbes Street. You're going to go through every paper they have — and that's a lot — for the past year — no, make that three — and search out any stories in any of them about a murder or stalking or even harassment that fits this guy's method of operation."

"And you?"

"I'm going to do the same at the paper's morgue. We get a lot of papers, and there are thousands of clippings in the files. We might cross wires, but it will also be an assurance that we won't miss anything. If you should find something, make a copy of the complete story and any follow-ups. If there's a story about an incident, make sure that there are names. We might be able to contact them. We can also try to go through any story with the reporter who wrote it or the cops who were involved. You should find more written stuff than me. I'm also going to contact news friends I have in smaller cities whose papers we don't get. Maybe they can help, maybe recall some similar occurrences. Maybe there are persons they know of who are being harassed at this time and can be warned. I will also try to contact some gendarmes in those places. Maybe they'll help us light up a bulb or two."

Bennett smiled and pointed to a rest stop turnoff. "I need a rest."

"Great. I need one, too, and we can get a bite to eat."

It was the strangest rest break Diane had ever experienced. The killer, if Bennett was correct, could be on his way to Pittsburgh at that very moment, and maybe at the same stop. God, she thought, he could be the guy standing next to her. He caught her glancing his way and smiled. She quickly turned away, stooped down, and pretended to find a lost object.

The thought that the man could be near them, gloating, continued to plague Diane. She used the restroom. Then she stood at a candy machine diagonally from the male restroom exit and scrutinized everyone who walked out, as if she could pick the killer out if he was even there. It wasn't long before she noticed people staring at her. *So I'm a pervert*, she said to herself, and beat a hasty retreat to their table.

Chapter 13

Diane checked her watch as they turned onto her street. Ten o'clock. She covered her mouth and yawned. "Boy, that was a tiring trip. I'm glad I was able to get some rest."

"You weasel. At least you were able to sleep," Bennett said.

"You're mad because I didn't drive."

"Not exactly. Well, yes. But next trip, no matter where we go, you're the driver." After a few seconds of silence, Bennett continued. "Anyhow, I'll call you in the morning."

Diane's handbag had been in the space between the two front bucket seats. Bennett lifted it to hand it to Diane. "Holy hell, what's in there, gold?"

"Just as good." Diane chuckled as she extracted her forty-five automatic. "I go nowhere now without it."

"The damn thing is huge. Wouldn't a Derringer be better?"

"Like hell. That wouldn't stop anybody. Let anybody try to screw with me, and you'll see what this can do. And remember, I know how to use it."

Bennett laughed as she slowed down to turn into Diane's driveway. She noticed the car while Diane was tucking the gun back into her purse.

"Diane. Whose car?"

Diane was startled for a second, but relaxed as she recognized the vehicle. "Whew, you scared the hell out of me. It's my mom's.

For a second or two, I thought I was going to have to back up my boast."

She patted her pocketbook as she spoke. "But, wait a minute," she said, glancing from the car to the house and back again. "Why's the house dark? Mom knew when I'd be coming back. Oh, shit!"

"Come on Diane. How could she know the exact time? It's late. She probably got tired, being all alone. Probably stretched out on the sofa and is taking a nap."

"Being alone; that's what I'm afraid of," Diane answered as she hurried out of the car and rushed toward the front door.

Bennett caught up with her just as she reached the stoop. A note was taped above the keyhole. Diane freed it and adjusted it so the rays of a streetlight made it possible to read.

"Oh, God," she muttered.

"What's wrong?"

Diane handed her the note and fumbled in the darkness for her key ring. She finally found it, but as she tried frantically to find the keyhole, the ring slipped out of her hand and disappeared into the darkness along side of the slab-type porch. She hurried down the steps, went to her knees and scraped the ground under the thick bushes in a desperate effort to locate it.

Meanwhile, Bennett held the note up to the light.

"Oh, shit," she whispered as she read the note out loud: "Diane this is your pen pal and guess what. Time is running out for you. I don't know about this pen pal thing, but there's that damned time element thing again."

Diane found the keys and hurried back to the door, extra careful not to drop the ring again. Bennett restrained her as she began to push open the door.

"The gun," Bennett whispered.

"What?"

"Your gun, Diane."

"Oh, yes," Diane muttered as she extracted the weapon.

"Don't race in," Bennett whispered, straining to look over Diane's shoulder.

Diane nodded and slowly pushed the door open the rest of the way.

"Mom?" she called quietly. "Mother, are you in there?"

No answer.

Diane stood beside the door and reached around the jamb to flick on the lights. Three large lamps immediately illuminated the room. Bennett held her breath, and both women were shaking. They inched into the room. There was no sign of life. Diane motioned toward a bedroom. They moved quickly, but quietly to each side of the door. Diane turned the handle as silently as possible, stood to one side and pushed the door open with a foot. It was a move that her husband had told her about when he described house-to-house combat techniques. There was still no sound. She hit the light switch. Diane motioned toward the doors of the other bedrooms.

"Keep an eye on them," she whispered, motioning the gun in their direction.

Bennett tried to watch other doors but couldn't help staring in amazement as Diane got into a crouch, showing as little of her self as possible, and peeked into the room. Diane held the weapon at the ready in front of her, one hand cupped under the gun butt, the other situated at the grip and trigger. She then darted into the room in a semi-crouched position, spun to face each side and then relaxed. The room was empty.

She followed the same procedure for two other bedrooms. Each was empty. The kitchen opened into the living room; there was no problem there. Everything was in place. There was no sign of a struggle.

Bennett was sweating profusely. She ran the back of her hand over her forehead. "Well, she isn't in bed, so she's probably visiting a neighbor."

"It looks that way, but it's strange, because she hardly ever had much to do with my neighbors — and her own neighbors, for that matter."

Bennett laughed.

"Damn, Diane, you looked like some part of a SWAT team. Your husband taught you well."

"I was sort of hoping that he'd be here."

Bennett started toward the bathroom.

"I was just about to wet myself. As a matter of fact, I've perspired so much in the last few minutes that I feel like I've already done it. I'm soaked."

"Sorry."

"Don't be. Like the old saying, it's better to be safe than sorry."

Diane turned toward the front door. It was still ajar.

"God, Marge, we are stupid." she said, looking over her shoulder as Bennett neared the bathroom. She stopped as Diane pointed toward the open door.

"All that sneaking around and that shithead could have waltzed right up on us with ease."

Bennett was still laughing and making some appropriate remarks as she entered the bathroom. Diane turned her attention back to the front door but never got a chance to push it shut.

A piercing scream echoed from the bathroom. Diane stopped in her tracks. It was followed by another and then another. Diane whirled just as the bathroom door was smashed open. It crashed against a wall, hung awkwardly on one hinge for a second or two, than fell to the floor. A huge man, his left arm wrapped tightly around Bennett's neck, held her in front of him, some six inches off the floor. Her face was contorted in pain, agony and fear; she had taken the full brunt of the collisions.

The man was big, head and shoulders above Bennett. Long black and matted hair billowed and flailed across his unshaven face. His screams were an octave below Bennett's, but just as loud. His face was also contorted, but not in fear. He was slobbering as he screamed and cursed. Eyes, wild, dark, and piercing, seemed to be bulging until the pupils looked no larger than black dots. A thick scar ran the length of the left side of his face from his brow to below his mouth. It was more than prominent because it completely separated a heavy eyebrow and then continued across his mouth so that it appeared that he had a hair lip. It was the first thing Diane's eyes fell upon despite what was occurring; it was so ugly.

The man tightened his huge arm around Bennett's neck. Her screams were reduced to gurgling gasps. Her eyes bulged and her face was turning blue. They smashed into furniture as they stumbled across the room toward Diane and the front door. Bennett's body absorbed the brunt of the force as they smashed into Diane's china hutch. Dinnerware, silverware, vases, anything that was the least bit loose, flew in all directions. The noise was deafening. Diane was petrified, unable to move, as the fantastic hulk and his prisoner bore down on her. The man flung Bennett into Diane as though he were tossing a large teddy bear. The collision drove Diane backwards, hurling her sprawling onto the sofa. Bennett bounced off Diane, smashed into a nearby desk, ricocheted back into the end of the sofa, and fell to the floor, where she remained motionless.

Eyes bulging, teeth clenched, moaning, the man, just a few feet from Diane, reared his head and extended his arms toward her neck. Another ungodly loud and long growl echoed throughout the room. Diane stood up on the sofa and backed up against the wall. There was nowhere else to go. The weapon was still in her hand. She pulled on the trigger but nothing happened. She pulled again, this time with both hands, still nothing. Then she became paralyzed with fear. She tried to scream, but couldn't. She gasped for breath, her open mouth prevented any sound from escaping. She was going to die. She was sure of that. Bennett was already gone. But the man stopped. He glared at her for seconds.

"No" he screamed. "I'll be back. It's not your time." He pointed a finger at her, backed quickly toward the door and was gone.

Diane was unable to move for long minutes. Her chest felt as though someone had tightened a belt around it, and she bent over, fighting to catch her breath. Finally, sliding down into a sitting position, she stared dumbfounded at the front door. "Oh, God," she cried over and over.

Bennett groaned.

"Oh my God, you're alive." Diane's words were somewhere between a mutter and a groan as she tried to talk, but her words were hardly recognizable.

Bennett finally struggled to a kneeling position. She massaged the front of her neck with one hand and leaned heavily against the sofa with the other. Raspy moans intermingled with gasps as she tried to regulate her breathing through a trachea that had been close to being crushed.

"Diane," she finally gurgled.

Diane rolled off the sofa onto her hands and knees and crawled to Bennett. Her hands touched blood that had smeared the carpet. Diane stared at Bennett's clothing and then at the palm of her hand.

"My God Marge, you're bleeding."

Bennett shook her head as much as possible. "No," she gasped.

Diane looked at her hand again. "But, you are."

"No," Bennett managed again in a hoarse whisper, her head shaking vehemently back and forth. She tried, but was unable to say any more. She put a hand to her neck in a vain attempt to alleviate the pain and help her produce the words she wanted to say.

Diane reached for her, but Bennett pushed her hand away and drooped her head so that her long hair hung well down, almost touching the floor.

"It's okay. He's gone. It's over."

"It's not," Bennett agonized, the words tearing at her throat. "Your mother." The words were followed by a loud groan as she fell back to the carpet into a fetal position. Her sobs were uncontrollable. Her body withered convulsively.

"Oh, God, no." Diane struggled to her feet and stumbled toward the bathroom, gripping anything for balance, her head shaking, denying what she already knew to be true.

Her mother was in the tub, propped in a sitting position. Her head rested against the rear, rounded part of the tub, so that it was turned toward the door. He eyes, wide open, stared blankly at Diane. She was naked and covered with blood. It pooled in the tub around her legs. A butcher knife was lodged deep into her chest just below the neck. Her entire body had been mutilated.

Diane staggered back against the splintered doorframe, trying desperately to keep from throwing up or fainting. She screamed again and again as she fell, then struggled to her feet and staggered back into the living room. She bounced against a wall and lost her balance. Unable to break her fall, she crashed heavily to the floor, banging her head against the edge of her coffee table. It opened a gash. Blood poured over her forehead.

Earlier, as she had tried to help Bennett, she placed her gun on an end table. Almost blinded not only by blood running over her eyes, but also by an uncontrollable rage, she fumbled for the gun. It was then, as she pressed the trigger, that she realized why it hadn't fired earlier. The safety wasn't released and the gun wasn't cocked.

Reeling dizzily, Diane screamed the worst curse words she had ever heard as she released the safety. With each curse she pulled the trigger. An explosion, than another, and another, followed a curse. The bullets smashed into walls, furniture and one continued out into the darkness. Finally, the magazine was empty and Diane hurled the spent gun across the room. It smashed into the China closet, destroying the last few undamaged pieces of glassware.

Bennett, still on the floor, screamed hysterically. She held both hands over the back of her ears and burrowed her face as deeply as possible into the pile carpeting as Diane fired.

Exhausted, Diane fell back onto the sofa, leaning her head against its back. She smeared blood over her face as she rubbed tears that streamed down her cheeks. It was only then that she became aware of the excruciating pain that throbbed throughout her entire body. She cupped her head in her hands and bent over. And just as quickly as she felt the pain, it subsided, and Diane slipped off the sofa.

Chapter 14

Diane's body ached. Her head throbbed. Everything was blurred, fuzzy and hardly visible. When she opened her eyes, just for a second or two, the excruciating pain in her head worsened. Painful throbs pulsated in concert with each beat of her heart. She wanted to soothe the ache by pressing fingers against her forehead, but couldn't lift her arms. They felt weighted down.

As she slowly regained some of her senses, she realized that she was on her back and no longer in her home. There was a steady vibration under whatever she was lying on. And as the mental shroud faded somewhat, she was finally able to see through squinted eyes, that somebody dressed in white was sitting beside her. She began to cry.

"Easy," a soft voice whispered. "Just try to relax."

"Am I in an ambulance?"

"You're in an emergency medical vehicle, and we're on our way to a hospital," a man answered.

"I can't move my arms. Am I paralyzed?"

"No. Your arms are strapped to a stretcher. It's to prevent possible damage if you move."

"Why can't I see right? Everything is blurred and I'm dizzy. I can hardly make you out."

"You took a pretty good crack on the head, must have hit a piece of furniture. You've got a concussion."

"God, I hurt. Can I have something for the pain?"

"I'm sorry, no," the attendant said as he checked her bandages.

"Oh, God, now I remember. Where's my friend?"

The attendant didn't answer.

"Whoever you are, where's Marge Bennett? She was in the living room with me."

"She's in another ambulance. She's going to the same place as we."

"How is she?"

"I don't know. Both of you look like you took a pretty severe beating."

"Where'd they take my mother?"

"Your mother?"

"My mom. She was there."

"I'm sorry. I don't know."

"Has anyone called my father?"

"You're asking questions I can't answer. I'm just a medic. They don't tell us anything. Our job is to give you immediate attention and then get you to a hospital as quickly as possible. I have no idea what went on. After you feel a bit better, I'm sure somebody will fill you in."

"You don't understand. Somebody killed my mother, then tried to kill us," Diane cried.

"Please," the attendant pleaded, "I don't want anything upsetting you."

"Do you know how stupid that sounds? My mother was murdered, cut to ribbons. My friend and I were battered and almost killed, and you don't want anything upsetting me?"

"I'm sorry, I didn't mean it the way it sounded. I meant that you have to stay calm.

"That's just as stupid."

Diane closed her eyes. As short as it was, the conversation sapped much of her strength. Her weariness combined with the continuous vibration of tires running over the concrete roadway, caused her to drift into a hypnotic state. The next time she was really aware of anything, she was in a bed in a hospital room, and a little later found that Marge Bennett was in a bed beside hers.

Their stay in the hospital was four days. There were no broken bones, but due to the nature of the head injuries, they were kept for observation. Diane wished she could have stayed longer. Returning home would be difficult. She asked Bennett to stay with her and the offer was gladly accepted.

The police had concluded their crime scene investigation by the time the hospital released the women. Although the exterior of the house showed no damage, the interior was in shambles. Diane had no idea so much damage could be done in so little time. Most of the furniture was overturned, some of it broken. Pieces of glass and dishware were scattered throughout the kitchen and living room. The shattered bathroom door was still lying on the floor. Its jamb was splintered, its hinges dangling and bent out of shape. Sofa pillows, doilies and coffee-table books were strewn over the floor. Diane stood silently eyeing the damage, and then picked up a few pieces of broken china.

"God, Marge, this was my grandmother's. It was more than a hundred years old. Now, it's trash."

She tossed the pieces aside, then examined one of the holes where a bullet entered the wall. She stuck an index finger into it and shook her head.

"I wondered where these ended up. I must have been crazy."

"You were. It was the second time that night that I thought I was going to die."

Diane mustered up enough nerve to peek into the bathroom. She groaned and staggered a few steps backwards. The blood throughout the room had caked. Diane began to cry. Bennett guided her back to the living room and helped her onto the sofa.

"Don't worry," Bennett whispered, "I'll get it cleaned for you tomorrow."

They sat in silence for a while, then Bennett put water on for tea. They re-righted the furniture that was still serviceable and then sat at opposite ends of the table. Bennett poured the tea. Diane fumbled with her spoon. Bennett fingered the rim of her cup. Neither spoke. Finally, Diane stared for a few seconds at the ceiling, took a deep breath, squinted her eyes, ground her teeth and then looked directly at Bennett.

"Goddamit, Marge." She hit the table with her hand, then tried to shake the pain away. She pointed the index finger of the opposite hand at Bennett. "This is now a war. And I'll be damned if I'm going to end up like chopped liver. I will never let that son-of-a-bitch kill me!"

"That's funny," Bennett replied.

"What's so funny?"

"You."

"Me?

"Yes, you. How long ago was it when I met this petite woman, loving wife, quiet and unassuming, probably with no thought of ever harming anyone or for that matter of being harmed? She was just trying to have someone help her find her husband. Now, she's declaring war on a maniacal killer who happens to be a giant compared to her. Now that little lady, who looked as though she wouldn't hurt a fly, is ready to kill."

Diane nodded and laughed. It was a cautious laugh. "But it's really not funny. It's weird and frightening," she said. "I guess I would have already killed if I would have remembered to release that damned safety. That was really a disappointing and an almost deadly mistake. Now, like you, I'm sure that he's on some kind of schedule, and I can thank whatever his plans are that I'm still alive. I had the damned gun pointed right at him and could have ended this right there. But, I'll tell you what, Miss Bennett, if and when the opportunity presents itself again, panic will be out of the question. I 'will' be ready. And I guess I have changed, but after this is all over and if I'm alive, I'll change back."

"You think so?"

"I know so. It happens."

She then told Bennett how her husband had sometimes talked about how personalities of some people change temporarily. He once told her of reading about a Marine who had been in Viet Nam. He was quiet, never swore, vowed to never harm anyone and was planning to enter the ministry after his tour of duty. But in a severe firefight, his squad was pinned down by machine gun fire and several men — his friends — were already killed. This little guy, a feather merchant — that's what drill instructors called short guys like him — suddenly leaped up, zigzagged as he charged the machine gun nest, screaming and yelling like a banshee. He killed seven Viet Cong single handedly, wiped out the nest, and saved the lives of the remainder of the squad, and probably scores more who were coming up. His whole personality changed. But after it was all over, he sat down and cried like a baby. Under normal conditions, he would have never been suspected of being the type that would earn the Medal of Honor for bravery, let alone killing anyone.

"That'll be me," Diane said. "Nothing else matters in the world now other than saving us by killing this animal. Yes, I know, like you said, just weeks ago I would have found it almost impossible to even think that I could ever want to kill anyone, animal or human. But don't kid yourself, Marge, you will change, too. As a matter of fact, if he kills me and you get a shot at him, you'll kill."

Diane's mother was buried shortly after Diane returned home. The funeral was delayed due to an autopsy, which Diane thought unnecessary. It was evident what had happened. But Spinaldo, during a visit, explained how every detail had to be documented. When this man was brought to trial, every bit of evidence had to be there to convict him.

"He'll never live to get that far," Diane assured him.

The coroner's report revealed that her mother had been slashed thirty-seven times. But at that point, there had been no pain. The coroner concluded that she was unconscious, almost strangled to death before any knife wound had been inflicted. She wasn't raped. It was Spinaldo's theory, as he tried to reconstruct the event for Diane, that the attack was a surprise and took place in the bathroom.

"It appeared that your mother inadvertently interrupted the murderer while he was attaching the note to the front door. She was about to take a shower and was on her way to the bathroom when she heard a noise at the door. She was wearing a robe that was found in a corner of the bathroom. She went to the door, probably thinking it was you. Instead she caught the killer by surprise.

"She tried to slam the door," Spinaldo suggested, "and ran for the bathroom, which had the only interior door that could be locked. But that was futile. The door was forced open, maybe by a shoulder. Hard to tell, since the jamb, lock and handle were all damaged severely when he crashed out the opposite direction with Bennett in his grasp.

"Then, before he could leave, you and Bennett arrived. He was stuck in the bathroom, and any chance of escaping undetected was gone. Bennett entered the room and you know what happened after that."

When her father was notified of his wife's death and how it happened, he suffered a heart attack. He was hospitalized during the funeral. Diane was saddled with all of the arrangements. Bennett was of great help, but it wasn't over yet. Her father returned home, but had lost the will to live. Despondency was the problem and no medicine could cure that. Diane hired a hospice person and wondered what else could go wrong.

They decided to commence their research as fast as possible. Time was of the essence, and there was a lot to get done.

Chapter 15

Getting the house back in shape was time consuming and tiring. It would have been nice to take in a movie and a late diner, but they were out of the question. Returning after dark was just asking for trouble. There was no way of knowing if the man would be watching or where he was. He had already said that he was making a call from a nearby booth. He had his favorite parking spot. And he knew the area well, and could be watching from any of a dozen places. So Diane got a Royalty game from the hallway closet, and played the challenging word game. It was a relief just to get their minds off what had transpired during the past few weeks.

It was 10 p.m. Diane was returning the game to the closet when the phone rang. She shrugged her shoulders. "Well, here we go again. Our friend."

"I doubt it," Bennett said.

"Wishful thinking. Who else would be calling at this time?"

By then the phone had rung four or five times.

"Whoever it is, they're persistent," Bennett said.

"Well, he isn't giving up, so here goes," Diane said.

"Diane," the voice was almost a whisper. "When I read the news story about your mother's death, I didn't like what I read."

"That's too bad. I didn't think you were intelligent enough to read."

"Smart ass, aren't you? I didn't like the story because it didn't cover everything. She wasn't dead or unconscious when I cut her up, and neither will you be."

"You slimy bastard." There was little fright in Diane's voice. She was as calm and matter-of-fact as she could make it. She continued before he could say anything. "You're a smelly, stupid pig. That is what you reminded me of when you were here, a slobbering pig, and we had to get the house fumigated after you left. And cutting me up will never happen. You can bet your dumb ass on that, and also that I'll have the pleasure of watching you squirm after I shoot you smack in the crotch. I missed the chance before, but I won't the next time around. You should know by now that your messages, or calls are no longer bothering me in the least."

There was no sound at the other end of the line, as if it might be the first time any of his intended victims dared to talk to him in that manner. Diane continued. "Come over now or any time, you cruddy bastard, if you think I'm not serious."

She heard a growl, but not quite as loud as those she heard when they were attacked.

"You slut. You bitch. I might just do that." He was screaming "I'll come over and drag your ass into the bathroom and give you the same kind of bath your old lady got."

"We'll meet again," Diane answered, and then hung up.

She flopped onto her sofa.

"Oh my God." She closed her eyes, tilted her head back and tried desperately to catch her breath. "I can't believe I talked to him like that. I was shaking in my boots. I still am."

"Bravo! I'll bet that shocked the hell out of him. What'd he say?"

"That Mom was alive when he cut her and he'll be doing the same to me."

"That's bullshit. He's just tryin' to get under your skin."

Diane closed her eyes. She shook her head and began to cry.

Bennett sat beside her. She rubbed Diane's shoulders. "Come on, you did great." After a while, she helped Diane back into a sitting position. She didn't say anything more. She put an arm around Diane's shoulders and held her close.

"I'm trying to act tough, but I can't go on with this," Diane whispered between sobs. She used the edge of a cushion to wipe away tears that trickled down her cheeks. Bennett didn't answer. "I just can't. I talk big, but it's like a game. It's like he knows exactly what I'm doing and when or where I'm doing it. There's no way I can win. First Ron, then Mom, then my father, who will never be the same. And who'll be next? Me, I know that. But why should you be part of this? It's impossible. I've thought a lot of how you could have been killed or how one of those bullets could have hit you or a neighbor. I can't go on living like this. I just can't. This bravado stuff is bullshit. I have guns all over the place. I have metal doors and peep holes. I talk a big, but every time the phone rings or I hear footsteps outside or a car stopping, I come close to wetting myself.

"Does that sound like someone who should challenge a fanatical murderer? How long can this last? How long can my sanity last? I think I'm half insane already. All I do is think about this day and night. I wake up in the middle of the night and the first thing I think of is this maniac. I go to the store and stare at every man I see. Is he the one?

"Marge, maybe if I were as strong as you, I could handle it. But I'm not, and if he comes again, I'll probably not have enough strength to even pull the trigger, even if the gun is cocked. I'm kidding myself, and you. I'm walking dead lady, so why should you go through any of this? Just clear out. Just clear out and let me alone. And you know what? You'll still get a good story out of it."

"Diane," Bennett started, but was cut short.

"One time you suggested that I move. Why? He'd find me no matter where I go, I'm sure. And wherever I hide probably wouldn't be as safe as behind my own four walls. And how safe will that be? How safe was if for my mother?

"I remember once when Ron trapped a raccoon in our garage. They're dangerous when trapped, so he put weapons within easy reach no matter where he was in the garage, ax handles, shovels, logs, anything. He chased that critter for hours. He even shot an arrow at it. Finally got it. He could do that, but not me. I have weapons all over the place, so wherever I am, I have a weapon virtually at my side. If I'm on the toilet, one's on my lap. I even have one with me when I'm taking a shower. It's hung on a hook. All that, and I still think I wouldn't be able to use the damned things."

Bennett got up and stood over Diane. "Let's have another tea."

"You didn't hear one word I said."

"The hell if I didn't. I listened, but there's no way I could fathom how you feel about your losses. That would be impossible unless I went through the same thing. But remember, I came damned close to getting killed, too. I'm not about to quit and besides, he won't forget me now. He's said as much. And I can't let you quit. You're upset and as corny as it sounds, I don't think your husband would want you to quit either. We are not going to sit back and let this creature do us in.

"I'm glad you got that all out, but you're wrong. You'll see. If and when the time comes, you'll do exactly as you threatened. I do know that this petite housewife that I met at a police station is stronger than she thinks. And maybe neither of us will have to do anything if Spinaldo finds him first.

"Lets drink up and get to bed. Tomorrow, bright and early, we start our research. I'll work through everything I can at our news morgue, and try to link up similar crimes, and where and when they occurred. You hit the library. Like I said, there are newspapers from all over the country, so don't rush through them. Then ask the librarian for any type of magazine that might cover that same kind of story. Like *Time* or *Newsweek*, but no *Enquirer* type rags."

She took a last sip of tea. "You done with yours?" she asked Diane.

Diane closed her eyes for a few seconds, took her last sip, got up and let a long breath escape. She felt better and smiled. "I'm done. I'm ready, and I'm fine."

Chapter 16

It was years since Diane had done any library research. She had no trouble finding the newspaper current issues section, but using a computer to locate past issues was something else. Systems she had used in college no longer existed, and she was not a computer person; they frightened her. She had no idea how to operate the new system, even though there were directions on the screen. By the third step, she was totally confused and envious of others around her who seemed to be having no problems at all. She needed help.

"Information about murders?" a librarian replied to Diane's question. Unable to suppress a grin, the librarian tossed sweeping open palms to indicate the entire library. "Anywhere you look, from Shakespeare to Spillene."

"Very funny. I do not mean novels. I mean murders that have occurred during the past few years, like robbery murders, rape murders and especially serial killer murders. Show me how to bring news stories about murders up on the computer. I'm not familiar with library researching any more, and I'm trying to find a serial killer. That's why I'm here, not to joke around with you. I hope to find articles that might suggest where and when he might strike next. You could be of great help. We think that accounts of murders in papers from other areas could reveal something that will help us."

"I'm sorry. I shouldn't have teased you. Please forgive me. Just trying to break up the boredom. Are you a detective?"

It was a perfect opportunity to assure all the help she needed. Diane leaned over the counter. "Yes," she whispered. "I am a detective in the Pittsburgh Police Department, and like I said, we think that perhaps accounts of murders in some of the papers you have on file may help us discover something, a clue, anything that might help apprehend this killer."

From then on, the librarian could not have been more cooperative. She apologized several times for her behavior, and then walked Diane through every step of the way on a computer.

Pretending to be a police detective reminded Diane of the times that Ron had told how people loved to imagine having been a part something, especially if it sounded exciting and mysterious, and how most would believe almost anything they were told. She remembered his account of how his father had snowed a fellow ex-Marine who had been on the first wave at Iwo Jima into believing he, too, had hit the very same beach at the same time. It netted him a night of free drinks and a tremendous hangover. But more important, it gave the man an opportunity to find someone who really appreciated what he had gone through as a Marine and for his country.

It didn't take but minutes for Diane to get the hang of digging out news stories. Besides articles from major newspapers from the past three years, there were items from smaller city newspapers. The librarian returned almost every half hour to see if Diane might need help.

"Everything's fine," Diane answered at each visit.

During one visit the librarian sat on a chair at an adjoining cubicle. "Gosh, your job must be exciting," she said.

Diane continued her charade. "Sometimes, especially when somebody's trying to run you off the road or taking a potshot at you." She was using descriptions of typical scenes both had probably seen on most any television crime show. Diane shook her head slowly, puffed her cheeks and slowly released a long stream of air to emphasize the everyday perils she experienced.

"God, I'd give anything for a life even close to that," the woman said, her eyes following the rows of books that bore witness to the tedium of her job, and probably her everyday life style.

"Well, you have to not be afraid of ugly situations, and also to be able to shoot at somebody without too much, if any, hesitation. There's always regret or remorse. Sometimes it's not a pretty job."

"My God," the woman whispered. "You're so young and beautiful. Nobody would ever expect you to be a detective. Do you carry a gun?"

Without saying a word, Diane eased open her purse, providing a peek at the forty-five. It was more than enough to convince the woman that Diane was one of the most interesting and exciting persons she'd ever met.

Diane had a short-lived pang of remorse when the woman smiled and returned to her counter. However, the game was a bit of a tension relief for Diane. Then she turned her attention to the job at hand. She went back three years in each paper, searching every page for any article about women who were murdered or raped. With the exception of finding one article that didn't seem pertinent, it was boring work and she welcomed a lunch break.

The librarian, eating with friends at a nearby cafeteria, saw her entering. She excitedly waved Diane over to their table.

"What the heck did I get myself into?" Diane muttered quietly.

"You'll never believe this," the woman began.

"Uh, uh," Diane interrupted. "Loose lips sink ships."

"Oh, yes," the woman answered. "That was famous during the Second World War. It meant to be careful what you say."

"We're old friends from a reading club," one of the people said.

Diane smiled and nodded, then ordered a sandwich and a cold drink. She ate in silence; amused at the conversation that suggested that the time spent reading books they chatted about were the most important periods in their lives. Diane loved to read, too, and it dawned on her that she hadn't read a book since Ron's disappearance. She envied those women almost as much as the librarian envied her. Diane smiled, told them she had to get back to work, nodded and left. She knew the librarian would spill her guts just as soon as she walked through the door.

"Oh, well," she said as she approached the computer, "I've made her day."

She 'made' every day for the entire group when she lunched with them, since through their veiled conversations it was evident that the librarian had told them, and probably with much embellishment, about her search mission.

Diane found numerous stories of rape and murder, but it wasn't until the second day of searching before Diane found articles that meant anything. They were in *The Cleveland Plain Dealer* and ran for several days. The articles outlined how a woman from the west side of the city was found raped, mutilated and murdered. Diane made copies of the story and follow-ups. There was no indication of any arrests. It was an exciting discovery. She jotted the date of the murder across the top of the copy — December 13th. The husband had disappeared exactly 60 days before that.

Two days later, she found another story in a March issue of the Los Angeles Times. That article depicted events similar to those in Cleveland and her own situation. It was more detailed than that in Cleveland, and described how the woman was hounded for weeks before she was murdered. The timeframe was similar to that depicted in the first article. The murder occurred on March thirteenth. The husband was reported missing exactly 60 days prior to the murder

It was getting exciting. During three more days of searching, Diane found four more rape-murder stories. One was in Plymouth, a small town in New Hampshire; another in Chicago's south side. There was one in Columbia, South Carolina, and the final one in Denver. All four had the exact time spans as those she found earlier. She concluded her newspaper search, but she couldn't help but to wonder how many newspapers, to which she had no access, carried similar articles.

It seemed as though Bennett hit the nail on the head when she suggested all the murders were committed by the person who was planning her demise — and on a definite time schedule. She was anxious to compare notes. She was also anxious to determine her date with death.

"Well, that's about it," Diane said, as she approached the main desk.

"Did you find anything interesting or helpful? You've done a lot of copying."

"Oh, yes indeed, and you just might have helped us track down a murderer."

The woman was extremely excited.

"Do you have a card?"

"Somewhere in here," the woman answered as she eagerly fumbled through a drawer. "I don't get much of a chance to hand many of these out."

"Well, I'll keep it, and when we catch this person, you'll receive a letter of commendation. I'll see to that."

"Oh, wouldn't that be fantastic! Oh, God, wait till my friends hear that."

They shook hands and Diane talked to herself as she headed for the door. "She's as happy as a lark. That's probably how happy Ron's dad made that ex-Marine feel by sharing some of the fellow's battle experiences that nobody else cared about hearing. So there is good in everything, even in snow jobs. And madam librarian will get a commendation — if I'm alive to see to it."

People were staring at her, and she realized that she had been talking out loud. She smiled.

"Just running through some lines for a Broadway play I'm starring in." They watched Diane all the way to her car.

"I'm getting pretty good." she muttered, "First a detective, then a Broadway star. Everybody now has something to talk about at dinner tonight. We've all had a happy day. Ron's father would have been proud of me."

Chapter 17

Diane and Bennett met at Diane's home early the following morning. Diane placed a card table next to her dinette table, using both as a surface for sorting notes. There were a number of small bundles, and it took several hours to sort and coordinate all the information from the library and newspaper morgue. Diane was surprised that she had more information than Bennett, but Bennett explained it away. Much of the morgue files were of incidents within a relatively close proximity, while Diane's covered the entire country.

"Okay, I've been twiddling my thumbs for a few days. You had a hell of a lot more to search through than me. So, let's take a look at what we have. We've got to combine this stuff on incidents we've found and then separate all of them into chronological order. I hope then we'll be able to determine which ones, if any, are definitely connected with your situation. I'll lay odds that we're gonna come up with some useful stuff, and I'll bet it will lead us right to the murderer."

"From what I found," Diane said, "it sure seems like there is something going on, and maybe it's like you said; the same guy is like a traveling salesman of death and he's doing it on some kind of time schedule."

"Which one's first?"

"No. Who's on first? Which is on third," Diane answered with a laugh.

'Okay, cut the comedy."

"Okay. Couldn't pass the Abbott and Costello opportunity up. Cleveland's first."

Bennett spread their notes and clippings into separate piles.

"We'll read each and every story again," Bennett said. "You read those I found and I'll read yours. Maybe we'll find something the other missed. Take your time. We don't want to miss anything."

"Like what?"

"Like how the hell would I know? Just read."

"Snippy, aren't you?" Diane said as she set her forty-five on the table.

"Do you have to do that?" Bennett said.

"Do what?"

"Have that gun right in the middle of everything?"

"I thought I made it pretty clear that I'm not gonna get caught with it out of reach. Want to see how fast I can pick it up and cock it?"

"Never mind. There are enough bullet holes in this place already. The next one might be through my head. Just read."

It took several hours for each to read and coordinate the articles. Duplications of wire articles in which much of the coverage was similar were separated and set aside. Remaining were the most informative articles and a decent chronology of the incident written out on a yellow business tablet.

"Actually, the first story is about the murder itself and the follow-ups are interviews with friends, relatives and police," Diane said after she got hers sorted.

"Damn, you're observant as all hell. What did you expect, the interviews before the murder?"

Diane shrugged.

"Just trying."

"Sorry."

"That's okay," Diane laughed. "Here's an article that includes a photo of the woman and the print under it says she was 52."

"The cut line."

"The what line?"

"The cut line, not print. The cut line is what you read under the photo. That's what it's usually called."

"Gee whiz. You're going to make a reporter out of me no matter what, aren't you?"

"Maybe, but not as good as me. Now, let's get serious and back to business. What else do we have?"

Diane handed Bennett more articles.

"The case is still open. As a matter of fact, it seems that none of the cases I found have been solved."

"That means this guy is really crafty," Bennett replied. "He leaves no clues to his identity, and that's pretty good, considering how many times he returns to the same area. This woman must have gone through hell. She was stabbed repeatedly and mutilated. The coroner indicated she was sexually assaulted."

Diane handed Bennett another article. "Her family said she'd been bothered, more like harassed, for some time. They thought the police should have done something, but didn't."

"Again, what could they have done?"

Diane shrugged. "It seemed they could have done something."

"Just what I said. What could they have done? What did the police do for you until your mother was murdered? And what have they got so far? What did the police do for you other than answer your calls? What could they have done?

"Now they've got Joe Spinaldo, and a few honchos, working on the case, but I'll bet they've got nothing new. I'll also bet that unbeknownst to you, Joe has a police car buzzing by your place on a regular basis. But I don't think they could afford the manpower to have someone planted here all night long. Even if they did patrol or watch continuously, how long would it last? The guy's been around. He knows what's going on, or at least much of what's going down. Then one day they call the surveillance off, and the next day, guess who is tap, tap, tapping at your door? It won't be the raven. It's a tough situation for everyone involved."

"Guess you're right."

They went back to reading.

"You know what's strange?" Bennett asked after a few minutes.

Diane looked up.

"The age of the victim. She was 54."

"What's strange about that?"

"In the time that I've covered police situations, rapes in particular, this one just doesn't jive."

"Why not?"

"Usually, and I'm saying usually because there are always exceptions, if someone stalks a woman with intentions of raping her, it's somebody younger, like a good-looking dame like yourself, who excites every guy who sits beside her on a bus, or stands behind her in a grocery line. It's hard for me to remember many — if any — times where an elderly woman was stalked for sex.

"Even older guys stalk younger women. The only exception I could think of would be if a rapist stumbled onto an older woman, like your mom. But then, that's not stalking and harassing. There's something strange here is what I'm saying. Let's make sure we check the ages of other victims."

"What are we going to do when we get all of this put together?"

"We'll categorize it, present it to Joe, and see what he wants to do or can do. We're definitely gonna need him."

Diane agreed. Then she picked up her gun. "Do you have one of these?"

"Nope. Why do you ask?"

"Don't you think you should have one, since you are in on this up to your rear end? By now, this guy probably knows where you live. Like, what if he shows up and you're alone? I've got extras and you're going to learn how to use one of 'em. I'll teach you."

"Never mind." Bennett took the gun from Diane and hefted it. "If what I learn from you is how to handle a rod like you did when that guy tried to choke you, I don't need your help. Besides, I already know how to use one. What you could have done that night, or any night, was to have cranked the forty-five, then released the hammer back in place, slowly, so that all you'd have to do is pull the hammer back with your thumb, pull the trigger and shoot the bastard. There'd already be a shell in the chamber. So maybe Ron didn't do as thorough a job of teaching as he should have. So from now on, do what I just said to do."

"Where did you learn how to use a 45 like that?"

"My father. He spent four years in the Marine Corps. He taught me, but it was mostly for fun, like target shooting. He liked shooting and had nobody to join him, so I was chosen. I'm still leery of handguns. It was just for fun, but now it might come in handy for something beyond that.

"I'll be damned. So now I have a Marine-trained bodyguard."

"Yes you do, and I think we've jested enough for the kind of problem we have. So, once again, let's cut the bullshit and get back to work."

"Yes, sir!" Diane snapped, and saluted. "But I'm still gonna give you one of my guns."

"Okay. I'll carry it. Now, let's talk about what the relatives had to say."

"I know it's the same guy who's bugging me. It's gotta be. There are the calls, taunts, notes, and one relative even mentioned a mysterious car. That's the car hanging around here, and it sure is scary since it's not owned by anybody in this neighborhood."

"How do you know?"

"I've driven all over, a half mile in each direction and at different times of the day. I've never seen it. That car is not from here. It belongs to the maniac."

"Or to one of his victims," Bennett said as she shuffled through the papers to find a date. "When did this Cleveland woman get killed?"

"I have it. December 13th, one year ago. And the husband was killed exactly 60 days before that. If we solve this, you could write a series or a book. That is, if we live through it."

"Oh, thanks. I needed that."

"Well, sooner or later, we're going to come face to face with that possibility," Diane said.

"Okay, what else do we have?"

"Not too much other than more stories on the investigation which led to nowhere and no arrests. And that sounds like another trip."

"No trip," Bennett replied. "But I am going to call a Journalism friend who works at the *Cleveland Plain Dealer* to copy and send me information on the murder besides what was in the paper. Then I'm going to try to talk with the officer — I know him — who investigated the crime. His name is Mark Fleming and I happened to have double-dated with him a couple times when I visited my friend. Hopefully, he'll send copies of the official investigation — highly improbable, but not impossible. There's stuff in a police report that you will never see in a newspaper. Let's get on with it. How many cases do we have?"

"Six, counting Cleveland," Diane said. "That's fantastic when you consider how many more there are like this we know nothing of."

"Okay," Bennett said. "Maybe it will help us piece this together more accurately. Let's get crackin'. Can I use your phone?"

Bennett picked up the receiver without waiting for an answer and placed a call to the Cleveland Police Department. After talking to several people, much pleading, and calls to two precincts, she was able to find and talk with Fleming. She detailed Ron's disappearance and events that followed. It was difficult for Diane to listen about Ron's disappearance, his possible murder, and no less difficult hearing about her mother's death.

"So, Marge, you guys are playing detective," Fleming said.

Bennett quickly explained how she came across the story in the Cleveland paper, and they were following it up to see if there could be connection. She also told Fleming they were working with Spinaldo, and assured him they would contact Spinaldo right away if there was any substance to their search.

Fleming knew Spinaldo. One of his people had worked with him for a short time on a narcotics case that involved both cities. "A good police officer. Tell you what," he continued. "I'll have our secretary dig out as much as she can and fax the stuff to you. The case is still open," he said. "We have a man on it, besides myself, but like so many other cases, it's no longer top priority. We've exhausted every lead, and there were hardly any to begin with.

"We need luck now, somebody who saw something and comes forth. But I have to insist that the information does not leave your possession."

After the conversation, Bennett went to her office, waited for the material, then returned to Diane's home. The package contained photos, and Diane slowly shook her head as she viewed some. "My God, other than the face, it could be the woman in Detroit," she said.

"There's no reason for us to look at any more," Bennett said, and began putting photos aside. "We already know what the others will look like."

Diane held Bennett's arm. "No. Leave them out. I want to look and hate until I'll feel nothing but complete satisfaction when I pull the trigger on that bastard. There is no doubt, this is the same guy."

"You're right,' Bennett said. She spread the photos on the table. The woman's head was almost severed. She had virtually been gutted. The same look of horror was frozen on her face, her eyes open, staring dead ahead. Diane recalled seeing a nineteenth century sketch of a cowboy pointing his six-gun straight ahead, and tilted up a bit so that they muzzle followed the viewer to wherever he moved. The woman's eyes had the same affect on Diane.

"Well, at least I didn't throw up," Diane said.

"Good for you. It's gonna hurt each time, and I wish there was some way to avoid it," Bennett said as she again set the photos aside.

The woman had been subjected to harassment very similar to that which Diane was experiencing. The husband, since he disappeared, was a suspect, even though members of his family described him as a loving person who cared for his wife. A number of others interviewed, described the couple's relations as ideal, even after some thirty years. There was no reason, they felt, why he would have killed her. The husband was still on the active missing persons file, but the writer was of the opinion that he was dead.

Someone had reconstructed the last hours prior to the man's disappearance. One of his daughters called early on the morning of his disappearance and talked to the wife. The husband was going to the market for some milk and a newspaper. That's the last anyone ever heard from him.

"Look at this. It's the same damned thing," Bennett said. She handed the sheet to Diane. "Read it. The time between his disappearance and her death was 60 days, and the calls started the day after his disappearance, with the caller saying just the person's name. Does that sound familiar?"

"Does it ever," Diane said, "and according to notes I have here, the police tried to trace the calls. No dice."

There wasn't much more they could do. It was late, and Bennett slept over.

Chapter 18

Diane's night was miserable. She was tormented by another strange dream. A huge, shadowy figure was chasing her in a dark vacuum. It was laughing and groaning and calling her name. Just as it was about to reach her, she'd awaken.

She'd try not to go back to sleep, but eventually couldn't help but doze off, and the dream would reoccur. It was during one of these sequences, just when the figure caught her and began shaking her that she screamed. She heard another voice. It was Bennett's, and she was doing the shaking.

"Hey, wake up."

Diane was gasping for breath and continued to struggle.

"Whoa, hold on." Bennett held Diane's arms until she relaxed a bit, than helped her into a sitting position.

"Look at you. You're soaking wet. I heard you screaming and it scared the hell out of me. But I'm a good scout," she said, as she hefted her gun.

Diane managed a smile as she ran her hands over her forehead and through her hair. She stared at the perspiration that coated her hands. "Good lord, it's like I've just taken a shower." She used the bed sheet which was already damp, to towel off.

"I've a hard enough time sleeping as it is. I'm awake every time a car goes by, and now I'm running into this."

Bennett handed her a robe as she described the dream. "I really think I've lost it."

"That's bullshit. Besides, we couldn't afford that. Anyhow, I was just about to wake you. Come on, breakfast is ready."

"The bastard chased me halfway through the night and finally caught me. Maybe that's some kind of a bad omen."

A few minutes later Bennett poured coffee for both of them. She took a long sip and then began to giggle.

"Screw you, Marge. What's so funny? I was scared worse than I was on my wedding night, and you're laughing."

"I really wasn't laughing at you. I just remembered how I used to get my sheets that wet, even wetter."

"You had nightmares?"

"Hell no," Bennett replied, tossing her head back and laughing harder. "My sheets were soaked because I wet the bed until I was about eight."

"You idiot," Diane kidded. "You had some kind of emotional or mental problem."

"That's for sure, and I must still have one, or I wouldn't have hooked up with you. I'm the one who should be having dreams."

During the meal, Diane again wondered how they could laugh at all, considering what they've both been through, and their possible future.

"I think I know what's on your mind," Bennett said, elbows on the table, holding her cup with both hands and looking over the rim. "We stand a damned good chance of being tortured, raped, murdered and then cut to pieces. And our mental problem is that we're stupid enough to sit here and giggle." Diane nodded. Bennett continued. "Maybe it's good therapy, but whatever, what will be will be, and what will be now is for us to get some work done."

It wasn't long after they finished eating that the telephone rang. Diane started up, but Bennett motioned her back. "Hold on," she said as she picked up the receiver. She didn't say anything.

"Diane?" the voice whispered.

"Yes."

"No! This isn't Diane," whoever it was shouted. "Where the hell is Diane?"

"Right behind me, you jackass, and we're discussing how I'm gonna watch as she shoots your testicles out past your rectum." Then she started laughing. "It'll sure in hell wreck-em."

"You bitch!"

Bennett laughed as loud as she could for a few seconds, cutting him off, and slammed down the receiver. She plopped into her chair, shaking her head. Her hands were shaking.

"Oh my God, I'm outta my head."

"It's amazing," Diane said.

"What? Him?"

"No. You. You've just now assured yourself that you are in this as deep as I am."

"Hell, I was in this for sure the second time I met you. I just had a feeling that day that something was drastically wrong. Besides, he already told us I'm also on his hit list, so what's the difference?"

"But you shouldn't even be involved."

"Maybe so. But I am. Besides, like we decided, if we live, the story will be a hell of a money maker."

"At my expense."

"No. I hope it's at his. I'm not going to sit by and let anything happen to either of us. If the ending goes as I just told him it would, that's about the best climax, other than sex, that anyone could ever come up with. And we'll share the proceeds."

Diane stared straight ahead for a couple of seconds, shaking her head slightly. "I sure as hell wish I could be that sure of things."

Bennett chuckled. "Don't kid yourself. I'm not sure at all, but it beats thinking about what could happen. I meant what I said, but if that weasel could have seen how I was shaking, he would have had the last laugh. I am continuously scared. This rough front is nothing more than a façade, so now we've both acted tough. Besides, if we don't think that way, we'll never be able to act that way — or any way for that matter. Oh boy, I wish we could disappear to Katmandu or some other God-forsaken place."

"Why?" Diane answered. "He'd find us."

Diane motioned toward Bennett's hands. "They're still shaking, but what the hell? I shake every time I think about this whole situation. And that means I shake all the time. It doesn't make sense. Why me? Why did he have to kill my mother? Why Ron? We never did anything to hurt anyone. Ron was tough, real tough, but he wouldn't hurt anyone. He didn't have any enemies. I've seen him back away from short sawed-off runts, those small guys who always think they're tough. He could have decked any of them with one smack. But he never did. Who could be this mad at us? Why were we chosen?"

"That's the catch, right there," Bennett said. "I really don't think he is mad at you or was mad at Ron personally. Something has kicked him off and we have to find what that something was. Why is he killing these people? And, if he is on some kind of schedule, like we think he might be, why? And then there's the job of finding out how much time we have left. Actually, all we have to do is to add sixty days on to the day your husband disappeared."

Bennett reached for her purse and extracted her gun. She waved it slightly. "No telling from where he called. Could have been around the corner. And since I gave him a hard time, we should keep these handy because there's no way in hell that he's gonna bust in here and surprise us."

Diane moved one of her weapons from the kitchen counter to the table.

It wasn't long before the phone rang again. Diane started toward it, still harboring slim hopes that it could be Ron, but Bennett restrained her.

"It's him. Let him suffer. He knows we're here, and not answering will really piss him off. Let's get back to work, but keep the guns ready."

The dishes were dumped into the sink, and within an hour materials from the next reports were sorted into neat piles.

Diane stood up, stretched a little, than moved toward the front window.

"God, I'm getting tired of reading this stuff," she whispered. "It's depressing." She parted the curtains and stared out for a few minutes. She shook her head, brushed away a tear and returned to the table.

"You all right?" Bennett asked, started to get up.

Diane waved her back.

"I'm alright. I miss Ron, and I know I'll never see him again."

Bennett sat quietly. She ran her tongue over her teeth, looked up at Diane, than toward the ceiling, perplexed. She took a long deep breath.

"What?" Diane asked.

"I don't know. Before, I probably couldn't have really known what to say or how you feel, but now I think I'm at least a bit closer."

Diane sat back down across from her.

"As a reporter, other than writing properly, I never gave a lot of stories a great amount of thought," Bennett said. "Maybe I should say afterthought. When I wasn't personally involved, it was something I might sympathize with and feel for, but I was still far removed. There's deep and sincere empathy, but often not even time to think about it, or that it could happen to me. It's a news item, so you get on with your writing — facts and interviews about the event — and then on to the next story. You think about it for a while and then it's gone.

"But it sure takes on a completely different significance when you become personally involved, not just covering a story, not just facts from a police blotter or interviews. You suddenly realize that you could be the one they will be writing about next. You realize that those sentences you've typed across the page so many times should have been more than just grammatically right words. Then you start thinking about your next story, and you decide that it won't be just finding out what happened and merely categorizing it. So many of us do that. We were always taught 'just the facts', and so many of us have failed to really understand, to relate properly how someone's life and hopes, everything they planned for later that day, or week, or year, were destroyed. We write about the impact of the sorrow and the futures of those who are left, but again, it's almost the same selection of words for every incident. Then you realize, like I'm doing now, that you've done all those stories not journalistically wrong but not entirely right, and wish you could rewrite every one.

"What we've seen and have gone through also makes me think about the cops in homicide, and others who handle these things. How could they do it every day and avoid becoming full of hate and bitterness? They're up to their knees in it all the time, and then I suppose they imagine their own wives or children as victims. The stress and hatred, and fear, has to be near impossible to keep under wraps, and yet most of them do. It builds a thundering silence. Just look at us now, almost walking with our backs toward each other; guns are all over the place. Sometimes I feel like just screaming, and I feel so sorry for those cops. And I feel so sorry for what that beast is putting you through."

"Putting both of us through," Diane said, "but I guess we did enough screaming that day to last for a lifetime. How could we ever forget it, especially if or when we'd marry, or remarry in my case. Every time our husbands leave the house, we'd relive all of this."

She tapped her fingers nervously on the table. "Talk about ever needing a shrink. But let's get off this and move on."

"You're right. Whatta we have?"

Chapter 19

"Los Angeles," Diane said, as she shoved a stack of news clippings across the table. "If this one's the guy we want, at least he's not a racist. This victim was black."

She walked around the table and spread some of the articles.

"Look at this one. It states that this woman's husband disappeared the same way Ron did: just gone. He worked in a hospital. The day he disappeared, co-workers said they saw him talking to another man who they had seen him with a few times before. The two men were in the hospital's parking lot."

Bennett listened while she scanned another article from the pile. "And look here," she said, as she ran an index finger over the article as though the sentences were printed in Braille. "This one tells how they also described the man as burly and with a beard and dark hair. If that doesn't fit the bastard who was here, then I don't know who else it could, be unless he has an identical twin brother who's just as sick."

Diane nodded. "Friends and relatives said the man who disappeared was a great guy, had no enemies and was a devoted family man. And yet, police considered him a prime suspect because he was gone. That's like saying Ron is doing this to me."

"But didn't you think, at least for a while, that Ron might have been the one calling?" Bennett didn't wait for an answer. "Police also go on the premise that people, friends or relatives, do not always know what's going on behind closed doors. That's why the first ones they look at are family members. There are many murders committed in families that appeared to be rosy, but in reality, were anything but that."

Bennett pointed to a later paragraph in the article. "Two months," she muttered.

"What?"

"Two months. Doesn't that ring a bell?"

"Yes it does. Sixty days. Here we go again," Diane said. "Two months. Just like the others. This guy kills the husband, and two months later finishes off the wife. Forty-two, black, two children, and one of them was also murdered. And the police think he also killed the child. Doesn't that sound like it could have happened the same way as it did with my mother? Mom interrupted the killer. We interrupted him, and that poor boy must have done the same."

"Yeah," Bennett said. "You know, this guy is no dumbbell. He is way ahead of the police. He makes each murder seem as though it's the result of a crazy family blowup where the husband goes bonkers. The police theorize he did lose it, maybe after years of abuse by his wife, even though their relationship always looked great to others. Whatever love they had apparently turned into hatred, so much so that the husband's only desire was to punish his wife for the abuse he had suffered. He goes berserk, and cuts her up, finishes her off, and then disappears. The cops search for the husband, while our guy safely keeps his appointments with another victim in another city."

Bennett leaned her elbows on the table, her chin in her hands, and sighed. "Some day they'll have a computer system nationally that's sophisticated enough so they can feed information from all over into a central bank and come out with what we've been working our cans off to get and then more. I'll bet they'll be able to almost plot a course that will be so accurate they'll be waiting at the next intended victim's door."

"That seems a little far-fetched," Diane said.

"Not if you think about computer development over the last thirty or so years. As a matter of fact, the FBI is supposed to have that capacity, but I doubt if it's effective. Well anyhow, let's move on." Bennett pushed the articles aside and nodded to Diane for another batch.

"This one's from Chicago," Diane said.

"You know what that might mean," Bennett said.

"Let me guess. I'll bet it's another trip."

"You're getting smarter. Let's check the stuff out and see if it does add up to a trip to the great Windy City."

"What else?" Diane said. She handed a few of the articles to Bennett.

Diane slumped back into a chair.

"What's wrong?" Bennett asked. "What are you thinking of?"

"What if all this leads us nowhere?"

"Diane. Are you crazy? How could it not lead us somewhere? We'll find out whom if we keep on this path. One thing for sure, he'll find us if we don't beat him to the punch. So it's certainly going to lead us somewhere, one way or another."

"How's the grave sound?"

"Not too good."

Bennett pored over the Chicago articles, then waved one slowly as she spoke. "This victim was 26. Names Marie Latsky. Her husband, Lazlo, was a couple years older. He disappeared, and what else is new? Two months later, she's dead, chopped up the same way."

"Maybe we should get Joe into this thing now. It's really getting pretty hairy. We shouldn't have waited this long."

"I think so too," Bennett said. "Maybe it's because of the attitude of the other police people. But let's see what Chicago has to offer first."

Bennett spread a few more articles. "This didn't mean that much when I first read it, but look at this." She pushed an article toward Diane. "This time relatives, and not the police, were adamant about the husband being the killer."

"That's a first," Diane answered.

"Right. They said he was mean with everyone, especially with her. After he returned from the Gulf War, he disappeared."

Bennett began gathering up the articles. "No need to go any further with this right now."

"What are you doing?"

"Look," Bennett replied. "One of the articles describes the wife as being battered so badly on at least on two occasions that she had the police cart her hubby away. He even attacked the police. He gets out on bail. He's gone and later on, they find her body."

"Sounds pretty close," Diane said.

"Close isn't the word. Exact is. Lazlo Latsky is our man. I'd bet my life on it. What the hell am I saying?" Bennett laughed. "That's exactly what we are betting, our lives. But we are going to get the rest of the story first-hand. Get a couple days worth of clothes. Like I said, we'll see what Chicago has to offer."

"Where do you think he called from today?" Diane asked as she started for her bedroom.

"Don't know, but I'd bet it was from another city. If this stuff makes sense, he could very well be off taunting another victim or murdering one. You know, if he's been doing this since the Gulf War, there's got to be a lot more victims than what we've found. That's for sure since there are hundreds of papers that we never saw, and never will. He'll be visiting us again, but by the time he does, I hope we'll know more, and we'll also have checked in with Joe. We'll be ready for him."

"I've been thinking of something that we've seen over and over."

"What's that?" Bennett asked.

"The two months."

"Oh, yeah. When did this guy first call you?"

Diane shrugged. "I can't remember. I think it was two days — maybe even one — after I met you at the station. Yes, it was the day after he disappeared when I asked you for directions at the police station. I thought it was Ron at first. All he said was my name and then hung up. Later on he said something about his pen pal. I didn't understand that."

"Okay, we'll figure that out, and the exact date, when we get back. If he has you or us on his schedule, and we are sure by now that he has, then we'll have to figure out a way to surprise him. We have some time. But for now, let's head for Chicago."

Diane packed her clothes, than headed for the kitchen. She rooted through a cabinet drawer and returned with a handful of toothpicks.

"What the hell are they for?"

"Just watch," Diane answered as she followed Bennett out the door. She tested the door to make sure it was locked and then inserted a toothpick an inch from the bottom of the door between its edge and the doorjamb. She broke it so that it was barely visible, then spent ten minutes placing toothpicks at every first floor window and the rear door.

"Now, when we get back, if one of those are bye-bye, then we know we've had, or we have, a visitor."

"Not bad."

Diane pointed a finger toward her head. "I told you that zany bastard will never take me by surprise again."

"Hey." Bennett nudged Diane.

Diane's head had been resting against the side window. It had taken a while for her to become accustomed to the bumps and vibration of the car ride. But when she did, she had fallen sound asleep. It was costly. Her back hurt from stretching sideways, her neck was stiff and her right side felt as though it were paralyzed. She could barely lift her right arm. She had been using her right hand as a cushion between the window and her head.

"Damn," she moaned through a yawn. "It was so peaceful. Now I hurt all over. Just because I don't like to drive, doesn't mean you couldn't let me sleep."

"Quit complaining. I've driven a hundred miles and you never budged once."

"It's the best I've slept since our trip to Cleveland. No cars. No dreams. No phone calls. Just a pest who couldn't let me rest."

"I've been thinking. Here we are, heading to Chicago. We've been asking questions, talking to people, digging up articles and information, but I have yet to talk to one very important customer."

Diane raised an eyebrow. "Me, huh?"

"You're part of all this, remember? The star player, and if we are going to put something together, we should have started with you, so we'll do it now. We have plenty of time. I'll ask the questions, you answer."

"Shoot."

"Do you and Ron belong to any national associations?"

"Just in connection with his job, advertising and media associations. Ron belonged. I just tagged along for the women fun things they have at those meetings and conventions."

"Did Ron ever talk about friends in the Marines, like mental cases? Maybe he might have told them about you."

"He talked about crazy experiences and crazies, but I doubt if he talked about me much."

"First of all, service people like to brag about their gal or guy back home. We made our guys back home sound like super studs even when they were wimps. And it would have been easy for Ron to brag about you and flip a couple snaps around. Where did you go on your last vacation?"

"Atlantic Beach in Maryland. We were there for a week. Met a few people, got names but no addresses. Played cards with some of them a couple times."

"Did anyone come on to you?"

"Is the Pope Catholic? Yes, especially one guy, but none of them looked the least like the guy who tossed us around. Even I could have beaten this guy to a pulp. He was amusing, a mousy character. Always had a hand in a pocket. The women kidded that he cut his pockets out so that he could play with himself. He always stared at us like he was having sex."

Bonnet chuckled. "Sounds like one of my old boyfriends." Then she bit her top lip, frowned and nodded her head slightly as she tried to piece together questions that might lead to some kind of clue.

"Damn," she muttered. "What did you and Ron do that was unusual — other than in bed?" She chuckled.

Diane thought about the question for a few seconds. She shrugged. "Nothing. Not a thing. Anyhow, why are we talking about me and my vacations, when we know, at least think we know, who the guy is?"

"What if our guy isn't the guy? Then it might be nice to know where somebody else came from."

Diane answered the question again. "Nothing that I can remember. When I come to think of it, my life could have been classified as boring, although at the time, I didn't think of it that way. It sure isn't now."

"Okay. Think again. Something you did together."

"Movies, trips, dinners and for a while, a couple letters."

"Letters? To whom?"

"You know. Nobody in particular. Friends from school."

"Anyone else?"

Diane closed her eyes, scratched her head. "Let me see," she said slowly as she ran an index finger and thumb across her brow just above her eyes. "Oh, yes. There were a couple happy time letters."

"What the hell are happy time letters?"

"That's what Ron and I called a few letters we wrote to soldiers during the Gulf War. People were writing, if you remember, to help keep our service people's morale high. You didn't have to have a person in mind — just send a letter — a few nice words — and it ended up in the Gulf. Anyone of thousands of service people would get them. Nothing much."

"Yeah. So, other than those you mentioned, you wrote to no one else?"

"Right."

"Damn," Bennett tapped fist against the steering wheel. "There's just got to be some connection somewhere. This hasn't been productive at all."

"Right. So you could have let me sleep."

"You can go back to sleep. Oh, yes. I have to tell you, I had to get time off from my regular beat and also ask for enough money to foot this investigation. That means I had to confide in my editor. He's been on my ass, figuratively speaking, about where I've been, and he knew something was up. So I filled him in on exactly where we've been and what we're doing."

"So now, it hits the papers after all."

"No. That would give the whole thing away. Not only would we never find this guy, but other news people will get on it and probably botch it all up. I swore him to secrecy until we can bring this to a closure. He salivated when he heard what we're into. He's having our obits done right now. Just kidding. But it won't hurt, either, to have someone else in on all of this just in case — well, you know."

"Yes."

It took less than fifteen minutes in Chicago's third precinct station for the word to spread that two beautiful reporters from Pittsburgh were at the homicide division. It was no accident that officers who seldom were involved in that area found urgent need to be there. Within a short time, Bennett and Diane had three offers for a date. Bennett accepted a double date from the officer who provided the file on the murder, over Diane's objections.

"Come on," Bennett insisted after the officers had left. "No harm can come from it. You and I both need some companionship other than each other. And I don't think you should start feeling guilty or remorseful either. Besides, they're both hunks."

"That's easy for you to say."

Diane sat quietly for a few long seconds, finally taking a deep breath. "No," she said. "It wouldn't be right."

Bennett shrugged and squinted but didn't argue. She understood. "Okay, so let's get back to work."

Most details were the same as the other they had read about, and similar to what Diane was experiencing. After they recorded the names and addresses of those who were involved and those who were interviewed, including the parents of the victim, they returned to the motel and watched a movie.

Chapter 20

Parts of Pittsburgh might have been similar to what they were traveling through, but Diane had seldom seen them. She stared in silence as they wound through Chicago. They could have been back in Detroit, she thought. Beautifully maintained houses lined a street for one or two blocks; pride of ownership, as Realtors would say. Then, for the next two or three blocks, homes were decaying or boarded up. Attractive properties would reappear, and the changing scenery continued that way for what seemed like miles.

Many streets were lined with junked cars, windows broken, interiors stripped, wheels missing or tires flattened. Garbage and trash were strewn on sidewalks and streets. On some curbs, trash bags or open garbage was piled two or three feet high. What was more surprising, and disgusting to Diane, were occasional sightings of rats rooting through the garbage while youngsters, unconcerned, played just yards away. Most of the occupied houses had iron bars across storm doors and windows.

"Is it that unsafe that they have to be virtually imprisoned in their homes?" Diane asked.

"They feel that way, and so would you after you've been ripped off three or four times, scared stiff by someone trying your door at two a.m., or saw a neighbor killed by stray bullets. The tragedy of installing bars is that residents, trying to keep safe, sometimes become unsafe. Kids get trapped inside when their homes catch fire while parents are away. But don't kid yourself; there are places in Pittsburgh just as bad."

Diane shivered just thinking about it.

Gangs occupied most corners. Some members were black, some Chicano, a few white, some mixed, some older, some just youngsters. A basketball game was in progress at a few corners. Teams went at it, while others waited to take on the winners. In many cases, the basket was nothing more than a bottomless bushel basket nailed to a utility pole, or a regulation rim, minus the netting.

Diane lost track of time, mesmerized by the sights, until Bennett braked to a crawl and inched in behind a parked car.

"We're here." She put a restraining hand on Diane's arm before opening the door. "I know these kinds or neighborhoods, so here's what we do. Keep a tight rein on your pocketbook. Loop it around your shoulder. Don't leave it in the car. The windows would be busted the purse would be gone as soon as we turned our backs. It would be best, too, if we keep weapons and wallets in our pockets.

"These kids are very unsociable. You've just got to be as tough, or tougher, than they are. It's almost like an animal encounter. Show a dog you're frightened and he'll up and bite the shit out of you. Show him you're not, and chances are you'll walk away with a new friend. That's the way most of these gangs are. They are like dogs. Sadly enough, they're growing up exactly as their parents did. It's a hand-me-down culture."

She squeezed Diane's arm to emphasize her next point. "But there are some real thugs who don't give much of a damn for anything or anyone. Whether you show fear or not, they're just as apt to whack you. Keep extra alert and a hand on your gun."

Diane thought Bennett was exaggerating but quickly found differently. A basketball game at the nearest corner was stopped as opponents watched them drive by. They whooped, yelled, gestured and pointed toward the car. Diane and Bennett were no sooner on the sidewalk before a gang member, slouching, with hands pushed deep into his pockets, sauntered toward them. He was smiling, and kept looking back over shoulder toward his friends, who egged him on with gestures and lewd remarks.

"He's probably the leader of the pack," Bennett said.

"Look what we have here," he shouted back to his gang, "two live ones."

When he was fifteen feet away, Bennett turned and took a step toward him.

"Stop right there."

"And what if I don't?"

She pointed a finger at him. "Then this could turn into a nasty situation."

"Is that so? Maybe for you, but not for us." The words were lazily drawn out. He laughed and looked back toward his gang.

Bennett distracted him with some more banter while she flipped open her wallet. She flashed her driver's license. The pocket it was in had long before been trimmed in gold with a badge-like design on one end, causing the card to look like police identification. She used it many times and became good at moving it so that it was difficult to tell whether it was an official police I.D. or not. Those at whom she flashed it were always reluctant to ask to see it again, she later told Diane.

"Yes, sonny boy. Screw with us, and I'll just go ahead and plant a dum-dum right where you'll lose your manhood."

She shoved the wallet into her left pocket and pulled her gun halfway out of her right pocket. She spoke slowly and smiled, as though she would thoroughly enjoy carrying out her threat. The youth held both hands waist high, palms out, and backed off. He knew a woman, cop or no cop, would never be convicted of killing a mugger, especially in that neighborhood.

"No harm meant, ma'am. Just wanted to welcome you to the neighborhood."

"So now you have. Go on back to your playmates."

After he was on his way, Bennett turned to Diane.

"Where'd you ever get a police I.D.?" Diane asked.

"It's my driver's license trimmed up a bit. It never fails, and it gets me into — and — out of a lot of places."

After that, they had no problems.

Most of the people they wanted to interview lived close to the victim's residence. Everyone's conclusion was similar. The husband killed his wife and was hiding out.

"He was a mean, ignorant and arrogant bastard," a balding and bulging next-door neighbor told them. "Like, one time that crud was pushing his wife, Marie, around on their front porch, not too long before she was kilt. She was pleading and crying, so I went over and suggested he back off a bit. The sum bitch never says a word. He just turns around and pops me one."

The man opened his mouth and placed an index finger and thumb over his front teeth as though they were still loose and he could wiggle them.

"See this? It's false. The real one stuck in the sum bitch's fist. Then he turns right around and biffs her like it was her fault that I said something. She goes flat on her ass. I'm already on mine and we're there, facin' each other. So, her blood's squirtin' outta her nose, and mine's squirtin' outta my mouth. It's all over us. I looked like a turned-over bottle of ketchup. Then the sum bitch bends over us, and spreads his arms wide like an ump does when a runners called out at home plate. 'You're out,' he yells, and laughs like hell. That's about the fifth time he's arrested for sluggin' her and the fifth time he's right back out. You won't believe it, but the stupid broad, after he keeps knockin' her for a ten-yard loss, always withdraws any charges and pays any costs. I would a let his ass rot in the clink if I was she. She'd probably be alive today if she did."

"Did you file a complaint?"

"Whatta ya think, I'm crazy? I'd probably be dead now, too."

"Do you think he might be dead?" Diane asked.

"Hell no. But lots a people 'round here sure'n hell wish he was. There's a lot of people 'round here with missin' choppers just like mine. They're scared. That sum bitch is big and bad and if he comes back...." He raised an eyebrow and tilted his head, as the sentence tailed off. "There was only one good thing about having that animal around."

"What was that?"

"He was so ornery and mean, nobody screwed with us or our properties. It'll probably be open season on us now."

"Can you describe him?"

"Sure. Sum bitch is about six feet, two, probably two hunert 'n thirty pounds, has dark, shaggy hippy hair down to his ass when it ain't in a pigtail. Always wore dirty closes and smells like pig. How's that for a description?"

"Pretty vivid," Bennett answered, snickering as she eyed the T-shirt the man was wearing. It was also vivid; dirty and far too small, exposing his navel and a huge beer belly that hung well over a belt half-hidden somewhere under the overlap. "He does sound pretty bad," she added.

"Sister, bad ain't the word. He's a friggin' psycho."

Bennett thanked him as they walked away.

"This place would be a hell of a lot better if two broads like youse was livin' here," he called after them.

Several other neighbors had similar comments and descriptions of the man. Some also displayed scars as remembrances. The final stop was to the parents of the victim. They lived a few doors away and both were reluctant to talk.

"We've told everything we know to the police. I don't see how Pittsburgh would have anything to do with it. We'd like to put it behind us."

"I'm sure you would," Bennett agreed, "but you can't, not as long as her husband might be back at any time. Who knows whom he'd murder? It might be you. He might think you talked your daughter into a divorcing him. That could be bad."

Bennett managed to coax them into inviting her and Diane in. It took another half hour of casual conversation before the couple was completely relaxed. Bennett prattled on about returning to Chicago, where she had grown up and what the neighborhood was like. She talked about her childhood on Johnston Street, close to three miles from where they were. She described the neighborhood.

"It was called 'copper canyon' she said, because so many policemen lived in the vicinity." Soon, they were chatting like old friends. The couple knew the Johnston Street area, had friends there. Bennett never lived in Chicago, but a sorority sister did, and on Johnston Street. She had taken Bennett home many times.

She finally convinced the parents why she was trying to locate the missing husband. He might have been seen in Pittsburgh and was planning to kill Diane. They needed more information, what he looked like, how he dressed, and in-laws were the best source for that. Their cooperation might lead the police to him. And then everyone, including the victim's parents, would be safe.

Diane marveled at the ease with which Bennett concocted stories and situations — actually half-truths — and her ability to gain trust. After tearing Chicago down to Diane, she talked to the parents as though it were one of the greatest places on earth to live. *That's probably what makes her a good newswoman*, Diane decided.

The man was mean; that was for sure. The parents didn't like him from the start when their daughter first introduced him, even though he acted like a perfect gentleman. He didn't have the long hair or the meanness, they said. At least he didn't show it, but there was something missing, something that made them not like him.

"Call it intuition or what," the mother said. "He was a sham. There was something about him that wasn't telling the truth. But there was no convincing Marie, and for a while after they were married, we began to think we might have been wrong. They moved in up the street and she seemed very happy. But it didn't last long.

"He drank a lot and began to beat her. He lost jobs, actually got fired from every one. Marie always had some kind of bruise, and when we'd ask her about it, she'd always say she fell. We asked her how come she never did that before. Then I asked her if Lazlo beat her. She cried, and that answered the question. We confronted Lazlo one day, and believe it or not, he lifted me from under my arms and tossed me, yes, tossed me out the door. I hurt my back when I landed. He started after me. When my husband tried to restrain him, Lazlo took him by the back of the collar and the waist of his trousers, and threw him down the front porch steps. It was just like an old cowboy movie when they toss somebody out of a saloon's swinging door. My husband went head first down the steps. Got a concussion and a busted arm."

The woman's husband lifted his arm at the elbow and waved it to emphasize the point. "Damned thing never did heal right," he said, and started to roll up his sleeve.

"Never mind," his wife said, and continued. "Lazlo swore like I never heard anyone swear before, and he shouted that it was his house and for us to stay the 'eff' out. So we did. But when we were able to see Marie, we told her to see a lawyer. She refused, even though the beatings continued.

"Then he joined the army reserves. We didn't know why. He wasn't patriotic; didn't give a damn about our country. We thought he did it because nobody would hire him. But later, we found out that beer-drinking buddies had talked him into it: weekends they'd have, getting away, drinking up a storm, finding other women, and getting paid while doing it. But he got a big surprise. The fun ended when he was called up to active duty and ended up in the Gulf War. He was mad because he never expected that. And while he was gone, Marie filed for and got a divorce. Lazlo was notified while he was in the Gulf. The divorce was final before he got back.

"He was mad, like a crazy man. The first day he was back, he beat her so bad that she ended up in the hospital and he ended up in jail. He got ninety days and was ordered not to bother Marie and not to get near her again. When he got out, he was drunk most of the time day and night. But he didn't stay away. He called her and told her he was going to kill her. We told Marie to call the police and then hide. She didn't believe he'd go that far, and she paid the price. So did we. Our daughter was gone."

"And you think he killed her?" Bennett completed the story.

"Certainly. Who else? He said he was going to kill her. He's gone. No trace. Nothing. Sure he killed her. Not only that, but he mutilated her too."

The woman brushed tears away with her apron.

"Wouldn't you think he'd pop up somewhere?" Bennett muttered as she moved toward an end table and picked up a photograph. "Marie?"

"Yes."

"Very pretty. Do you have a photo of her husband anywhere?"

"We tossed every one we had in the garbage can. That's where he belonged, probably where he came from," the woman answered. She looked toward her husband who nodded.

Diane and Bennett thanked the pair and left. Bennett leaned against the steering wheel and placed her palms in a praying position over her mouth. She was silent for long moments, nodding her head slightly in agreement with whatever she was contemplating.

"I'm excited. We have our man." She eased out of the parking space. As she passed the corner, she waved to the boy who had greeted them. He flipped her a finger. Most of the gang followed suit, yelled and shouted obscenities at them. One mooned them.

"Nice kids," Diane said.

"Probably the kind parents in this neighborhood like to brag about," Bennett answered, and shook her head as though she was sorry for them. "Whatever. But, I am excited because I'm absolutely certain this guy, Latsky, is responsible for what we know about and probably for a hell of a lot more that we don't know about."

She pointed a finger over the steering wheel and moved it slowly back and forth. "And he's probably somewhere out there at this moment, doing the same thing. Now, we're going to start from the other end."

"What other end? Damn, Marge, why do I always have to ask questions with you?"

"So? You get the answers, don't you? Can't answer until one's asked. We know that somehow or other we've got to piece this shit all together and find the common denominator between you and all these others. And I think getting sent to the Gulf and his wife divorcing him, especially when he was away, precipitated all of this. I also think he was insane before that all happened. The sad thing is that he's going after someone right now, and we'll never know whom. But, we do know, for sure, that we are on his calendar of events."

"And that's why this whole thing is so insane, the common denominator." Diane said. "I've never had any connection at all with any of these people, and how in the world would Ron have met any, especially a crud like this character or his wife. And the murders are all over the country. I still think this is just a helter skelter situation. He's having fun killing."

"Oh, he's having fun all right. The question is, why is he having fun, and why is he going all over the United States to have fun? And if it were helter skelter, there'd be no schedule and you'd have been dead weeks ago. Why would he keep taunting you and the others? No, it isn't helter skelter. We've been thinking for a while that it's planned, that there is some kind of schedule, and that's exactly what it is. It's no longer a theory."

It was dark when they arrived at Diane's street. Bennett turned off the headlights as they entered the block. She parked a half block away from the house.

"We're getting smarter and smarter," Diane quipped.

"Oh yes. And get out as quickly as possible so the dome light doesn't give us away. And don't slam the door."

Neither had to be told to have their weapons ready when they reached the house. There was no sign of life and no lights. A check of all the lower windows and the back door showed no toothpicks had been disturbed. The stub protruding from the bottom of the front door was as Diane had left it. But they still were taking no chances.

Diane eased the front door open. Standing to one side, she reached around the jamb and flicked on the living room light. Bennett held her weapon, gripping it with both hands, chest high and pointed forward, ready to start firing at a moment's notice. Diane motioned for her to wait and hurriedly slipped through the doorway and to one side. Nothing. They checked every room, including closets, always aware of what happened the night they weren't thorough.

"Whew," Bennett sighed. "I bet your neighbors just love us. At any moment they could be in the middle of a Dodge City shootout. I wonder how many times we'll have to go through all of this sneaking in crap?"

"As many times as necessary if we want to stay alive," Diane answered.

"You're right, but I feel like Wyatt Earp, always having a hand on my gun."

Diane began to giggle.

"I'm scared half to death, and you laugh," Bennett said. "What's so damned funny?"

"You should know, from your Marine dad. Didn't you ever hear the saying about when a Marine calls his weapon a gun?"

"No."

"Well, they make this poor sucker, in front of all the other recruits, hold his rifle high with one hand, and grip his crotch with the other. Then he has to scream, 'This is my rifle and this is my gun. This if for shooting and this is for fun.'"

"Well, that's one of the finer bits of Marine lore that Dad didn't mind if I missed," Bennett answered as she headed for the kitchen.

"Let's have a cup of coffee and get a good night's sleep."

"You know what is really odd?" Bennett asked later as she fluffed a pillow and tossed it into place on the sofa.

"What?"

"How many movies have I seen where the cowboy hero bunked with his pistol under his pillow, and I wondered if that was really the way it was. But here I am, proving to myself that is was that way, and still is.

"Well, it must have made the cowboys feel better, because it sure does something for my peace of mind," Diane answered.

Bennett smiled as she pulled off her shoes feigning as though they were high-topped cowboy boots. "Goodnight, pardner, and happy trails to you until we meet again."

Diane tipped an imaginary Stetson and retreated to her bedroom, but there was one more surprise. "Marge," she yelled. "That son of a bitch!"

Bennett raced into the room, gun cocked. Diane was sitting on the bed, visibly shaken.

"What?"

Diane handed her a note and a toothpick. "This note was tucked most of the way under my pillow."

Bennett read it.

"This tooth pick will replace the broken one I took out of the back door. I have no trouble with locks; you should know that by now. And that stupid-assed trick is the oldest in the books. I just wanted to let you know that your time is getting close." The letter was accompanied by a Polaroid shot of one of his victims.

"How could he pick the lock and not set off the alarm?" Diane asked.

Bennett shrugged her shoulders.

"He probably did set it off. First, who would hear it? Isn't it just for you when you're inside? And show me the neighbor who'd want to get involved. Well, anyhow, he just told us time's not up, so I guess we can still get a good night's sleep, but make sure your gun's in bed with you.

"Oh yes," she added, "what bothers me is that the alarm is supposed to go directly to the police station, but he must be smart enough to know how to disconnect if from wherever it's hitched up outside. Like I said, I think he's smarter than we give him credit for, but we'll worry about that tomorrow."

Diane went to the kitchen, got two chairs and forced one under the handle of each exterior door. "If a lock won't keep him out, this will, and if it doesn't, at least we'll hear him."

Chapter 21

As another safety precaution, Diane and Bennett set a new procedure for answering either of the doors. Bennett would swing the door open and step quickly to one side. Diane would stand five or six feet dead center from the door with her weapon at the ready.

The plan was effective. They had called Spinaldo as soon as they got up about what they had discovered, and he came to the front door as their first visitor. Bennett swung the door and Spinaldo froze as he stared at the huge 45 in Diane's small hands. The barrel was pointed directly at his chest.

"Whoa. I'm the good guy, remember?" He quickly sidestepped out of her line of fire, as he saw in a second that the weapon was cocked and could go off with just the tiniest movement of Diane's finger.

"You expecting someone?" he managed past a nervous grin that failed to disguise how frightened he had been.

"We are always expecting someone," Diane said as she lowered the gun. "My boy friend called again in person yesterday."

"In person? He was here?"

"Body and soul. He's getting to be a regular visitor. He left a nice note, as usual."

Diane explained the toothpicks, and showed him the note and accompanying photo. Spinaldo put both into an inside coat pocket.

"I see a peep hole," he said.

"But I wouldn't see who might be standing beside you with a gun to your head," Diane replied. "Then I might have the unpleasant task of shooting through you to get to him. But now you know that I don't plan to be taken by surprise again."

"I guess not. Where'd you get the cannon?"

"Ron bought this. We used to fire it. But there's a cannon, as you call them, in every room, and some rooms have two. And at least one goes with me wherever I go."

"Licensed?"

"Who gives a damn about a license if I'm dead?

"Can I come all the way in now since I'm not the bad guy?"

"I'm sorry." Diane stepped back.

As Spinaldo entered the living room, he noticed the weapons in that room and the dining room. He walked to the kitchen. A 38 was on the sink board. "You weren't kidding."

"Damn right, Joe,' Diane said, as she led Spinaldo to an easy chair in the living room. She and Bennett sat on the sofa across from him. "If I waited for your police people to come speeding to the rescue, both of us would be dead meat."

"You know, Diane, if you have to stock this place like an arsenal, why don't you just move to a safer location?"

"Maybe Joe's place, Diane," Bennett offered.

"Now, that would be nice," Spinaldo said.

"Might be, but don't let your fantasies run away with you," Diane interrupted. "Anyway, we didn't call you for a Freudian encounter. And I'm not moving because it wouldn't do any good. He'd find me no matter where, even if I was at your place, and I think it's time now for someone to join us and that'll be you. We want to fill you in on what we've found."

"So you guys are still playing cops and you think you found the killer."

"Damned right, and doing a hell of a better job than the cops. We know who he is, but we haven't found him." Bennett retorted.

"Are you kidding?

"Do you think we called you over to play games? No, we are not kidding," Diane said.

"Great. By the way, before we get into that, where'd you get the guns?"

"The Hill District," Bennett said. "We stopped the car at a corner and asked a couple guys where I could buy some."

"The most dangerous area in Pittsburgh? Are you crazy? Don't you realize what could have happened?"

"Sure, we could have got killed, just like we might get killed by this nut case," Diane said, as she hefted her weapon. "Maybe I should have called the police to help us find some hot guns. I hope you don't think we were stupid enough to go there unprepared."

"How did you do it?"

"I pulled up, called one of them over and asked where I could buy eight handguns that work. He looked at me, smiled, big white teeth gleaming under the streetlight. 'I'll get you seven and one free if you give me one free,' he answered. But after we assured him business only, he said to come back in four hours."

"And you did."

"You see the guns, don't you?"

"You're lucky he didn't set you up. You're probably lucky you're alive."

"Really, Joe, do you think we're that dumb?" Bennett said. "What do you think we are, detectives?"

Spinaldo shook his head. "You like hurting people, don't you?"

Bennett continued leaving the question unanswered. "We snuck up on them 20 minutes early, lights out, to see if they were setting up to snooker us. We eased up about two blocks away and waited. I left a cross street between us so there'd be a fast turn-off in case of hanky panky. When I felt it was as safe as could be, I flashed my headlights from that distance. That way, we weren't in their midst. Diane still had her baby cocked and ready just in case."

"You sure have nerve, but you're a little short on brains."

"Before Ron disappeared, I would have never dreamed I'd even get close to going through anything like that, but things change," Diane said. "I've changed"

"Both of you are something else." Spinaldo laughed. Then he got serious. "Pour me a cup of that coffee I smell, and let's see what you've got."

It took several hours to detail everything that occurred, where they'd been and what they found out. After they concluded, Spinaldo sat silently for a while, than leaned back in his chair. He tilted it back far enough so that Diane made a frantic grab at it to prevent it from going all the way over.

"Don't worry. I've never gone all the way — the chair that is." He eased back to its original position, leaned forward, rubbing his chin. "You know, this is really fantastic."

"Is that all you can say?" Bennett answered. "We already know that. Tell us something new."

"Geez, I don't really know what to say. We considered this guy as a local psychopath."

"We think that's what police in 49 other states think, too," Bennett said.

Spinaldo dropped his arms so that his forearms rested on his thighs, hands folded. He looked toward the floor for a few seconds, then looked up slowly and continued.

"All of these and probably scads more that we probably don't even know about. Good lord, he's all over the country. It's going to be a bitch nabbing him."

"That's what we know and that's why we called," Diane said. "We are at a point now of getting him before he gets us. And we're sure we can help you do that. He's on a 60-day time frame, so now we've got to depend on you to really help us because we don't have much time left before he comes after us."

"I'll do what I can, but you know this is interstate, and we probably should be contacting the FBI."

"No FBI, at least not now," Diane said. "Those fools are dumber than the Pittsburgh police. They have egos as big as their rear ends. They'd scare him off for sure. Then I'd be living like this for years. Just about the time I put all the guns away, guess who'll be at my door. He'd be back sooner or later. So if you can't do anything other than what's happening in this state, work with us as though you think it is just in this state, and forget the FBI."

He shook his head. "I don't know. I can get in a peck of trouble if I keep this back."

"As far as anyone else is concerned right now, you don't even know about it," Bennett said. "And that's the way it will always be. If we get killed, you can pretend to come up with this theory and tell them you followed through exactly like we did. Who wouldn't believe it? Hell, we might even get you a promotion out of all of this; Chief of detectives or something like that. How's that sound?"

Bennett stood up. "We've called you and not the FBI because we think you can help us. All we have to do is set him up. If we can lure him into this area, then it wouldn't be an FBI situation. Lure or not, he'll be here. If we fail, we won't be around to worry about it, and you can go on just as we've suggested."

Spinaldo looked down, folded his hands between his legs, shook his head and took slow deep breaths for ten seconds. Then he raised his head slowly, looked at Bennett, then to Diane. He reached up a bit with an open palm and answered; "That means you want me to use you as decoys."

She nodded.

"I can't do that."

"Why not? What the hell are we now? It's the only way to catch him. He's too crafty otherwise, and he might outsmart us anyhow. Then it's back to the starting block and than the FBI."

"I'm really shaky on this," Spinaldo said as he went to the stove and refilled his cup. He returned and sat with his head drooped and eyes closed. He tapped the cup lightly on the table. Nobody spoke. He took a deep breath, looked up, and shook his head. "Okay, we'll give it a try. But both of you do understand how dangerous this is going to be."

"What else is new?" Bennett asked. "How dangerous is it when we almost get killed? How much more dangerous can it be other than him finishing it?"

"Okay. Just so you know, what makes this so difficult is that his field of operation is nation wide and most serial killers don't do that. The FBI has the wherewithal to cope with this kind of thing; local forces don't. Most serial killers stick to one general area, and they are tough enough to find, let alone a guy who has the means to hit anywhere in the United States."

"We know all that," Diane said.

"Where does he get the money?" Spinaldo asked.

"Joe," Bennett said, "we wondered that for awhile, and he's anything but wealthy. People where he lived barely make ends meet. You should see the neighborhood. It's rats, punks, and poverty."

"The only other source for his money is his victims," Diane said.

"Yeah," Spinaldo said, "You're right. How much money did your husband usually carry?"

"Not a lot. He used to kid about not being worth enough to get robbed, maybe twenty dollars or so. He was always afraid of losing his wallet."

"Credit cards? Did he carry many?"

"Don't we all?"

As they talked, Bennett hurried to the kitchen counter where a rectangular wicker basket was overflowing with unopened mail.

"Diane," she asked as she sifted through the pile, "when was the last time you checked your mail? Like bills?"

"Oh, God, I don't know. I'm so far behind. At first I looked for a note or letter from Ron. When none ever came, I gave up and just tossed mail into that basket. Ron always paid the bills so, by force of habit, I guess, I never gave bills a second thought."

"You're lucky your utilities are still on. There's probably warnings in the stack," Spinaldo said. He grabbed a handful of envelopes.

"The first thing we do is look through this heap for credit card bills and hope that they are dated after your husband's disappearance. Your husband has been missing, what, going on two months now?"

Diane nodded. "Just about that. The way we figure, we've only got a few more days, and that's what has us worried. Everybody was killed exactly 60 days after the husbands disappeared."

"Then we really have to work fast," Spinaldo muttered after opening several envelopes. "Ah ha," he exclaimed as he waved a bill and then laid it on the table. "There's a charge of a five hundred dollars cash withdrawal."

"And here's another for a couple hundred," Bennett added, pushing a bill across the table toward Spinaldo.

"And another," Spinaldo added. "So you were right, Diane. He either gets cold cash from his victims or credit cards, or both. That buys food and gas, and pays motel bills."

"But they ask for identification, don't they?" Diane asked.

"You go to a K-Mart type store. Who ever asks for I.D.?" Bennett answered.

"Maybe for a couple bucks," Diane answered, "but five hundred dollars is a little different than charging toilet tissue or stuff like that."

"Okay," Bennett retorted. "Go to a bank drive-in window. Drop in a request for a cash advance and put your driver's license — Ron's — in this case, in the tube with the request. Does anybody run out to check you out personally? See how fast they pour out five hundred smackers. If my memory serves me correctly, there's always a notice, sometimes as much as a thousand dollars can be collected from the window teller."

"So, what good is it doing to find all this out?" Diane asked.

Spinaldo sipped his coffee and leaned back in his chair. Diane wished he wouldn't. All she could see was the legs snapping. Then she thought *what difference would it make?* Two other chairs were destroyed during Latky's rampage.

"It's a little cold," he muttered.

Bennett refilled the cup.

"I don't know exactly right off hand," he said after a long sip of the fresh brew, "but a lot of things can come from it. Maybe it can give us a clue on his route. If we can figure out the time spans between each withdrawal, we might be able to nab him before he gets to you. We know when he's coming for his finale with you. I'd like to figure out when he arrives in town and where he'll be. Perhaps, after I go though these bills, we might have an idea how early he might be back here. Maybe the bills will show us if he has a favorite Pittsburgh motel."

"Joe, he is planning to come back on the sixtieth day," Bennett said. "We don't need any bills to tell us that. And I don't suppose he'd get here and hang around too long. I would think it's in, do the job, and get out. What bothers me most is why does he want to kill Diane. She — well it's now we — might die and never know why."

Spinaldo shook his head. "Hard to say right off. One serial killer victimizes prostitutes, another children and another gays. That's what they all have in common. I don't know when I last heard housewives as victims. That's too risky, doing it in settled neighborhoods. There are too many chances for a witness. And another thing, the great majority, as I said, sticks to one general area. For instance, Gary Ridgeway killed almost 50 people and hid their bodies near the Green River in Washington State."

"Yes," Bennett added, "and there was a guy in Detroit who killed prostitutes. His operation covered less than two square miles, but he killed almost a dozen people before he was caught. And another man up there murdered and sexually abused young boys, and he never did get caught. They think he died. If Latsky called it quits or died or got killed, we'd never know.

"But that's wishful thinking. I'd rather settle this once and for all. I don't want to live wondering every day about the possibility of him showing up. Here we have people from coast to coast getting butchered. They don't know each other. They never met. They are from all different races, religions, occupations, income brackets and ages. None seemed to be deviants or criminals. All the husbands disappeared and are presumed to have been murdered or the actual killers. And the husbands were all pretty nice people, except Latsky. Not a damned thing in common, other than being married.

"And nothing is happenstance with this guy. He selects his victims. He's picked Diane and a date for the execution. It's not like the prostitute or gay or child murderer. He's selected and stalked individuals. Those other murders were mostly random. And then again, why Diane? Why any of them? Why the mental torture and then physically taking them apart?"

Spinaldo took a long breath and a longer sip of coffee. He held the cup up to his lips with both hands, staring for long seconds over its rim as though the answer, like a message in a crystal ball, might come floating to the surface.

"I don't want to be slit from stem to stern," Diane said. "We have to figure out how to set some kind of trap."

"Damn. We've been way off base," Spinaldo said. "Our people, me included, thought maybe it was somebody who met you and made a pass. You rejected his advances, and this was a way for him to get even with a smart alec woman. But what you've told me changes everything."

"Wait a minute," Diane interrupted. "Marge, a while back when we were talking about this, you said you had an idea how he might select his victims. Tell us what it was."

"I have to make some calls first, and if they work out, I'll tell you what I hoped it would be."

"Well, now that we know who he is, or at least we think we know, I can go on that," Spinaldo said. "We've got to track him down, and I don't know how we can do that alone since this thing is country wide."

"Joe, please, I know what you're thinking, but no team right now. Maybe one more person right now," Diane pleaded. "If this doesn't work, we'll be out of it and you can get an army on it."

"My partner, Pete Zabala," Spinaldo answered.

"That's fine, but any more and you might as well get the FBI in," Bennett said. "Then he'll go underground if he suspects anything. Our advantage is that he doesn't know that we know."

"Boy, my rear end can really end up in a sling," Spinaldo said. "Diane, if I didn't like you so much, refusing would be a snap. Okay," he said only after another long pause, "I'll use my partner. Besides being my partner, Pete's a very close friend. He can keep a secret. But I still think if I confided in my boss, he'd go along. If we succeeded, he'd get credit for solving a countrywide killing spree. His hat size would increase by three sizes."

"You could still do that after this is all over. Both of you could increase hat sizes."

"I'm not worried about me," he answered as he started for the door. "It's both of you. I'll let you know where I am at all times. If Latsky calls or if you sense something's wrong, call me immediately."

He wrote out his cell phone number. "Memorize this. You might not have time enough to look it up. Meanwhile, I'll have someone watching out for you. And I'll also have a patrol car drive by as much as possible."

Diane followed Spinaldo to the door. She moved close to him. "Joe," she whispered, "thank you for not spreading this yet." Before he could answer, she reached on her tiptoes and kissed him lightly on a cheek.

"If you did tell anyone, it could mean so much more torture to go through. I like you," she continued as she gently squeezed his hand and kissed him again. She was trembling.

"Okay," he whispered, a bit hoarse. "I've thought of you a lot during these weeks, and I definitely do not want anything to happen to you."

"That was a nice scene," Bennett kidded after Spinaldo left. "Isn't love beautiful?"

"Shug up, pig," Diane quipped. "That's how one of my nieces used to say those words. She was three years old. Probably had more brains than you."

Chapter 22

After Spinaldo left, Diane began dinner. Bennett was in a bedroom making phone calls. She had been doing that for several hours.

"I got it!" she yelled, as she rushed into the kitchen. "I got it! I got it!"

"Got what?"

"I know exactly how you guys were selected and what everyone, you included, had in common."

Diane hurriedly set a bowl of potatoes she was mashing aside.

"How?"

"You remember your happy letters or whatever the hell you called them?"

"Yeah."

"Think about it. Happy letters. Our friend, ugly Lazlo Latsky was in the Gulf War. Wasn't that the only thing out of all the possibilities that we covered that could have been common among all of you? At least that's what I thought. So I called as many of the survivors of the victims as I could find, and guess what?"

Bennett excitedly answered her own question before Diane could say anything. "All of the victims, and or their husbands, wrote letters to GIs during the Gulf War."

"And?"

"All of you must have given a lot of personal information and unfortunately for a lot of people, this nut was the one who received or gathered up those letters after others read them. I called some Veterans of Foreign Wars Clubs, pretending to be a reporter for whatever their hometown newspaper was. They were glad to provide names of members who were Gulf War veterans. Out of the five clubs I called, I found two men who had received those kinds of letters. What they did was to pass them around so more than one soldier could read them. So when Latsky got letters, he merely picked and chose those writers he liked most or maybe least, as his victims."

"Why?"

"I don't know the answer to that yet, but let me ask you a couple questions."

Diane shrugged. "Go on."

'What did you include in your letters?"

"Just some chatter about how proud we were of them, and stuff maybe to pick them up a bit."

"Did you ever write any of them and mention where you lived and what you or Ron or both did?"

"Yeah, but not much."

"But you might have mentioned advertising and maybe your ages."

"Advertising, maybe, but never our ages or our address."

"How about other personal information?"

"Not much, other than Ron having been in the Marines."

"Did you mention when he was in?"

"Might have."

"If you did, that would have given a reader a hint about your age. Did you mention anything about family or not having one yet?"

"I think I did in one or two."

"Like how?"

"Well, I think I mentioned that when we have children I hope they never have to go to some foreign country to fight."

"So he knows your name, no kids, so that gives him an approximate age, Ron's profession in which he probably gets paid handsomely, and the city in which you live. So now all he does is check the phone book when he gets back and he's got your address, unless you had a private number. And even then, all he had to do was call all the ad agencies in Pittsburgh until he found one with a Ron Duval. Or maybe you put a return address, possibly by force of habit, on your envelope.

"Others might not have revealed as much as you. Or they might have intrigued him for reasons other than yours — money, or something personal that might have set him off. Anyway, Latsky was in the Gulf War, so he had to be the one that got letters from all of you and perhaps others whom he hasn't even contacted yet or are in different stages of their torment schedule."

"Okay, what's that tell us for sure?"

"It tells us that we look no further and that Latsky is without question the murderer."

"But we already know that," Diane said with a frown.

"Yes, but it does answer the question of why you are on his list." Bennett flopped into the easy chair. "What it doesn't tell us is why he hates all of you — enough to murder. That's heavy. Something happened in his life to cause him to hate and kill and use you folks for revenge and satisfaction. And the letters all of you wrote were like maps, showing him the way for easy revenge, a man to kill, a woman to ravish and maim and a source of money to use to go on to the next victim.

"I tried to call Joe but he's out on some other case, so I left a message. This has been a hell of a day, so whatta ya say? Let's eat out and walk around or even take in a movie. I haven't been to one for ages, and I think we both need a diversion or we'll go balmy."

"Good idea," Diane agreed, "only a comedy. I don't need anything heavy."

She suggested that they put the news clippings and other material they had showed Spinaldo away before they left.

"Let it go until we get back," Bennett replied. "I'm tired of looking at them for now."

The need for Spinaldo arrived sooner than expected. It was shortly after they returned from the theater. They completed their safety ritual, room by room. The phone rang just as they finished.

"It's probably Joe," Bennett said as she closed the door.

It wasn't. The usual "Diane" was soft and calm.

Diane almost hung up, but during the few seconds between his word and the time it would have taken to hang up, she recalled what they had talked about on the way to the theater.

Diane, except for one of the most recent calls, always played right into his hands, and that was getting them nowhere other than closer to the time when he would make his final call. He always expected her to lose control as she had done so often. That was the way it was with all of his victims, they decided. They probably all panicked every time he called. That's what he wanted, she decided, to control, to have the last laugh every time, to masturbate, either mentally or physically, as he taunted them, telling them what he would be doing to them on that final visit. It had to have pained his already disturbed psyche tremendously when Diane not only refused to be intimidated by his most recent calls, but had the audacity not only to challenge him but to threaten him as well.

The plan now was to engage him for as long as she could, hoping that it might lead to something he'd say that could offer a clue or clues as to his motivation, whereabouts, or what set him off, and hopefully what his plans were.

He cursed.

"You still there?" he continued, his voice demanding, loud and harsh.

"Yes," Diane answered softly.

"Still Miss Wise Ass, aren't you? Still gonna blow my balls off, huh? No more screaming?"

"Should I be screaming?" Diane strained to keep her voice as calm as possible, when she really did want to scream. "Isn't this getting to be old stuff by now? It won't be long before we meet again, I suppose."

"Oh, we will, bitch, we will," he shouted, following with a gleeful, wild laugh that ended with a hacking clearing of his throat. "It'll be sooner than you think."

'Pig,' Diane thought. But she had no intention of quitting. She was into her role and anxious to continue. It was the most challenging thing, she was sure, that could ever confront her: playing a game of cat and mouse with an insane killer.

"Tell me," she continued, hoping he wouldn't hang up as he had done before, "why are you doing this? Not only to me, but to the others." She saw Bennett, who was on the other line, furiously waving her hands back and forth and she knew she had said too much. It was too late.

"You fuckin' whore," he shouted. "What do you know about any others?"

"I know," she answered softly. "And I'm used to your vulgarity, so swear all you want." She started it, by a slip of the tongue, but now had to continue. So what if he knows what they know? As a matter of fact, she rationalized that it might open him up more than they hoped. "I also know that you've done this all over the country, and that it's on some kind of schedule."

"You whore," he screamed. "You dumb-assed bitch. You think you know everything."

"Not everything. And don't shout, you'll get your neighbors mad."

"Don't worry about any neighbors. Nothing's around me but trees."

Diane was suddenly proud of herself. He has to live in some secluded area. If only she could pinpoint where. Then she laughed. *How stupid. That whereabouts can be anywhere within millions of square miles.* Nevertheless, she continued.

"Are you going to run away, or are you going to tell me why you're doing this?"

There was no answer. She was sure he was about to hang up.

"Yes," came a calm answer.

He didn't say anything else, but neither did he hang up. Diane sensed he wanted to continue but wanted her to lead the way. It was probably the first time any intended victim had enough presence of mind to converse with him. She almost felt like the psychiatrist leading the patient. It was also confusing, and she shrugged as she turned toward Bennett, who was holding the other phone to her ear. She used hand gestures to coax Diane on.

"Well, are you going to tell me or are you just going to slobber some dirty words out and hang up?" They were the only words Diane could think of. *Not bad*, she told herself. This time her voice was demanding. She got a nod of approval from Bennett. Again, she waited. "Well?" she drew the word out.

The man's voice was high and shrill as he mimicked Diane: "Well, are you going to tell me or not?" He repeated it several times, then laughed. "You bitch, you're so damned smart. My wife was the same way. She ain't anymore."

Diane looked to Bennett and motioned toward the phone message recorder. Bennett nodded, and motioned with an index finger that it was already on.

"You mean Marie."

Latsky was quiet, stunned momentarily that she knew about his wife, but soon continued. "Yeah, I killed her. It doesn't matter that you know her name or mine. It won't do you any good. What did you do when your husband was away? If you're like my wife was, you were probably out taking on anybody you could get a hold of. Then when he'd come home, you'd give him a big-assed kiss."

"Did your wife do that to you?"

"Yeah," he snarled. "The bitch was shacking up all the time I was gone."

"The Gulf?"

"Gone, none of your business. That's where, just gone." He hesitated for a few seconds. "All my life, all I ever got from women was a bunch of shit." His voice broke. Diane was she sure he was starting to cry.

"My wife divorced me. And my mother, my own mother; she was worst of all. She hated me and I was a kid and I didn't know why."

He hesitated again. Diane could hear his quiet sobs. His words were separated and his voice often trailed off as he continued.

"Yeah, then I found out why. It was because of my old man. I never did anything to her, but it was him. She hated my old man. All they ever did was argue, and call each other ugly names, always starting with four-letter words. He'd slap her around and then bug out, sometimes for days, probably shacking up with some other bitch. So she takes it all out on me. Beats me, and keeps telling me that if she hadn't met up with my old man, she'd never had to put up with a retard like me. I'm not retarded. So how would that make you feel, bitch?"

He remained quiet, as though expecting Diane to comment. Strange, despite all he was putting her through, she began to feel sorry for the man. Nobody had ever come close to treating her like he had been, and she couldn't begin to imagine what it would be like, or how it might have affected her. When she didn't answer, he continued.

"You there?"

"Yes," Diane said softly.

"Then she starts screwing around with all kinds of trash, alkies, junkies. I mean, she brings them home and lays them in the living room, bedroom, on the floor, anywhere. And times when she was potted, the bitch even jumped into my bed with a couple of them, and I had to lie there, listening and pretend that I was asleep. I wanted to kill her, which I eventually did. I stuffed a pillow over her face. I was the only one at home, so everybody thought she died of a heart attack. And who was going to hold an autopsy on some sloppy-assed alky bitch?"

"So now you kill men and women and punish them just to prove how much you hated your parents and your wife," Diane murmured. "You're killing them just to get even, despite the fact that these people never hurt you, didn't even know you. How do you decide on who it will be?"

"Who gives a shit?"

"I do, since we were one of those who wrote to you."

'You're pretty fuckin' smart. How'd you figure that out?"

"Because we're pretty fuckin' smart, that's how. And your time schedule, that's pretty smart too, isn't it?"

"Yeah, it's smart. It's exactly how long it was from the time I got a letter from some shit-faced lawyer telling me that she dumped me until the time the divorce was final. If you could talk to the Chicago cops, you'd find that the lawyer is still missing."

"But you didn't kill her as soon as you got back, so why'd she stay?"

"Because I made sure her new boyfriend disappeared, and besides, she was scared."

"Didn't she question his leaving?"

"Sure she did, so I told her that I warned him and he bugged out. Knowing me, she bought it. She knew I'd kill him if he hung around. So I killed him anyway. Some stupid-assed judge told me I wasn't supposed to go near her, but I got stoned one night and went over to her house. I knocked her around a bit and then shot off my mouth too much, because she figured it out that I killed the guy and said she was going to the police. I told her if she did I'd kill her. I moved out but didn't wait too long before I decided that I should kill her fast, or end up in prison. So I did. Simple as that."

"You're impotent, aren't you?" Diane said.

"You bitch. What about all those women you found out about? Who do you think made it with them? You're just like my wife was, always mouthing off. She told me the same thing, but you'll find out what I can do. Didn't you get the word about your mother? Yeah, I raped her and it was fun, especially what I did afterwards."

Diane really wanted to scream. Instead she calmly concluded her end of the conversation. "You're full of shit. You couldn't satisfy your palm let alone a woman. You bastard, you'll get yours."

He let the threat go by.

"So you know who I am and all that shit, but it isn't going to do you a bit of good. I know you've kept me bull shittin' so your friend can trace the call."

"She can't trace it."

"Well, anyhow, I'm right down the street at a public booth, if that will help you. And I watched you go in. It's not time yet, but I'll be calling you again, soon, and in person and we'll see who gets who. Time's just about up for you and this broad that you're with. You can tell her that I have special things planned for both of you. And by the way, don't leave your news clippings lying around. The ones about me were interesting."

He hung up. Diane stared at the door and then the receiver for a few seconds before dropping it into its cradle. She turned toward the kitchen table where they had left the clippings. Neither had time to notice when they entered, but the clippings were gone. "Good lord, he was here again. That bastard was in this house again. He took all of our clippings."

"That son-of-a-bitch," Bennett answered. Then she checked the bedrooms. "The guns are gone. He stole all of the guns."

"Not all. We still have the ones we carry."

Bennett plopped onto the easy chair. Diane collapsed onto the sofa.

"He may be an ignorant bastard, but he's not dumb," Diane said. "But he's crazy, and he kills with impunity, like what's so bad about getting even. Well, anyhow, now we know for sure. God, it's amazing how so many things came together in such a short time."

"Yeah," Bennett agreed, "but even for the police, it often happens that way. It's like a light going on. They work, and search, and search some more, and then something happens or someone talks, and it all starts to come together. But we are so friggin' lucky that today wasn't his chosen day. Geez, how many times has it been that he could have been sitting in one of these chairs, just waiting to for us? I'm going to call Joe, right now."

Chapter 23

Spinaldo made sure Diane knew who was at the door. They weren't taking chances, and neither was he. They followed the same procedure: Bennett swung the door; Diane pointed the gun. Spinaldo looked at his wristwatch as he entered.

"Wow, one thirty." He apologized for being so late, but he recognized the urgent sound of their call, and figured they'd wait up for him. They all headed for the kitchen table.

"What will it be, beer of coffee?" Diane asked. "We've got some things to fill you in on."

"Beer sounds good," Spinaldo said as he selected a chair. "It's been a long day, a double homicide up in Oakland. I've been on the go all day. It feels great just to sit down." He finished the beer while Diane and Bennett described what had occurred.

"Whatta ya think?" Diane asked

"For sure, I think there's no way we can keep from getting our people in on this." His response disturbed Diane. It wasn't what she wanted to hear.

"What? Why?"

"Simply because any element of surprise is gone. The man knows that he's been identified. He knows that there's gonna be a huge manhunt for him. He knows, or will find out, that it won't only be here, but it'll be across the country, since there's no telling how many murders he's committed and where. There could be dozens of bureaus that have been baffled that will know who to look for. He knows there will be sketches or photos of him all over the place. There's no way we can, or should, keep this information from other police departments. As for us, we're way ahead." He chuckled. "We not only know who he is but also that he lives in some sort of secluded forested place which, luckily for us, narrows his hideaway down to some forty-five million sites.

"Funny guy."

"No, Diane. I'm only kidding. You both have done a hell of a job. Nobody else would have kept him talking like that. He revealed quite a bit. But, I can't keep this quiet anymore. Your slip about the letters assured that. Can you imagine what the repercussions would be if this wasn't reported and anything happened to you or others as a result? As it is, I'm going to catch hell and I don't feel like going back to pounding a beat.

"You also have to realize that he called from just a few hundred yards from here and that he was again in your home, and you didn't even know it until he told you. The toothpicks, new locks, or the alarm didn't mean a thing. Yes, he's no dummy just because he's ugly. And if there really is a schedule and this was the day, we'd be carrying you out of here right now in rubber bags."

Spinaldo played the tape again. Diane was surprised at how short the conversation actually was. At the time, it had seemed to last very long.

"What's amazing to me is that he talked so freely. The guy has had problems. He isn't backing down from his schedule. So, either he's really stupid, which I doubt, or he has confidence and assuredness by the tons. But, anyhow, I think the conversation did help," Diane said.

"We'll find out," Spinaldo said. "You're right, Diane. He isn't stupid by a long shot. If you think about it, he got information from you that can be helpful to him. You guys have done an absolutely great job, but you took a few hellish chances along the way, and I can't let that happen again. You've talked about a schedule. You say you had 60 days from your husband's disappearance. Now you have only a few."

"We know where we're at, and we are close," Diane answered on her way to the kitchen. She returned with a wall calendar, opened it to the month of May, and laid a finger on the thirteenth day.

"That's the day Ron disappeared. I had 60 days to live from then and we're almost there. All the husbands that we know about disappeared, and the wives died 60 days thereafter."

Spinaldo flipped the calendar to July and pointed to the thirteenth, which was already circled on the calendar. "That means there is less than three days before this maniac tries to kill both of you. It's a shame we didn't know about all of this before. It might have changed our whole approach to the case, and we might have had him by now."

"Like how? That's so easy now for you to say," Bennett retorted, "and it's irritating. First of all, we've really just put two and two together. But where in the hell have you and your people been? The police didn't have time for Diane. As far as they were concerned, she was, and still is, just another wife with a runaway husband. We see this all the time, so go home and wait. She heard that or something like it enough times to make her sick, or maybe just sick of the police.

"If two women playing detectives could figure it out, why couldn't someone in Pittsburgh's sterling police department, or you, for instance, do likewise? We started from scratch, and actually just until recently, plus today, became aware of the pieces that helped us complete the puzzle. I don't know why the police couldn't have done the same."

"Didn't you say you lucked out by accidentally finding a murder article in another city's newspaper?" Spinaldo asked. "Sometimes that's what the police need, too, a lucky break."

"Sure, I got the story of the mutilation murders from a paper," Diane said. "And that was luck. But isn't there a saying that goes 'The harder you work, the luckier you get'? Maybe whoever was on the case, especially after my mother was killed, could have been checking similar crimes in other cities or news articles, too. Maybe they might have come up with the same information as we.

But they're still looking for the guy who killed her and they can't get past Pittsburgh. So, don't try to make us heavies. You guys are the ones who are supposed to be the pros. Actually, by finding that Latsky is the killer, we might damn well save a lot of lives that would have been lost had this case remained buried for eons in some detective's desk."

The outburst disturbed Spinaldo. "This had all the earmarks of something and somebody local. There was no indication of anything widespread, even after your mother was killed. We can't go through libraries and whatever else you did every time someone is murdered in this city. But you are right in one respect. Finding out will save a lot of lives. Now let's skip this, and go on." He asked for another beer, took a long sip and ran his tongue over his teeth while rubbing the day's growth on his chin. He took a deep breath and went to the phone.

"He's probably staying at a motel rather than a hotel," he said as he waited for someone to answer. He told whoever was on the line, to start calling motels — the sleazy ones. He described Latsky.

"Put Zabala and anyone else that's available on it with you. Lasky will probably be using someone else's identification materials, so make sure you provide that description. I want the motel name and the name of anyone who checked in over the past couple days who comes close to that description. Jessie, it's a matter of life and death, so get on it right away.

"It's a hell of a long shot," Spinaldo said as he returned to the table. "There are tons of motels in or out of the city that he might be at, but we never know when Lady Luck will show her face, do we?" he said, a bit sarcastically while raising and eyebrow toward Bennett. He took one last long sip and started toward the door.

"There's not much more that can be done tonight. Just keep the doors locked, maybe prop the chairs again and remember, call right away if anything ... anything strange occurs."

He stopped at the door and turned around. "I'll have a man keeping an eye on this place within an hour. He'll watch out for you. Actually, since your friend likes to visit on wheels, and if he's already in town, he just might decide to park down the street again, so I think I'll plant my guy somewhere down there right away so he'll be in position should Latsky visit."

He muttered quietly as he started to leave. "If the chief ever finds out how I've handled this, I'll be busting my ass on some godforsaken beat up in the Hill District." He took a deep breath, looked back again at the women, smiled, shook his head slightly, and left.

"I think we pissed him off," Bennett said. "I wonder how he'd welcome a kiss from you now."

"He'll cool off," Diane said. "Right now, I'm ready for beddy-bye."

"Me, too," Bennett said, and began to prop chairs against the doors. Then she fluffed a pillow, tossed it on the sofa, and spread out a nearby afghan she'd been using as a blanket.

"Your sofa isn't the best bed in the world, but from now on I wouldn't be caught sleeping alone on my own beautiful king-sized bed for a million bucks."

She tucked her pistol under the pillow and flicked out the end table light.

Chapter 24

Diane listened to Bennett's heavy, steady breathing. She was sound asleep. Diane checked her alarm clock: three a.m. She was envious. She was dead tired, but she couldn't keep her eyes closed. Rehashing the conversation with Latsky didn't help. She couldn't let it go. Both she and Bennett were so calm and confident with Joe Spinaldo. It was an act. Diane was scared, more than she'd ever been at any time of her life. She knew Bennett felt the same. *Who wouldn't be,* she thought, *if they knew that within a few days someone was going to try to murder them?*

Less than three days to live. That is significant. She equated her situation to that of a person on death row who knew just when he or she was to die. She thought about Bennett. As a reporter, especially a police reporter, she had seen a lot of things go down, but as she said, they always concerned others. Now that she was personally involved, and in mortal danger, Diane wondered what Bennett's innermost thoughts were. Maybe she'd ask her in the morning. Her own immediate problem was how to get to sleep. She thought about sleeping pills but quickly ruled that out. She didn't want to be caught in some stupor if Latsky showed up.

Her thoughts drifted back to when she was at the police station, staring at the huge pillars. It seemed like yesterday, and she thought about her reason for being at the station in the first place. She thought of Ron. She knew there was no chance that he might be alive. She wondered how she could have ever thought that he might have been the caller? She failed to hold back tears that streamed down her cheeks onto the pillow.

She lost count of how many times she had cried herself to sleep. She closed her eyes, and envisioned Ron the last time they said good-by. He always smiled when he said goodbye, no matter how bad or mad he felt. He always said 'this might be our last goodbye.' She always wished she could be like that. Thinking of her husband intensified her hatred. Latsky took away what she loved most in life. He destroyed the beautiful existence she had enjoyed and turned it into a living nightmare.

She'd had often thought about death. *Who didn't*, she thought. Since Ron's disappearance, she wondered what he might be doing at that very moment. She had often wondered that about her mother.

Life had been so simple before. She and Ron were happy. There were few worries. The future looked great. Ron was on his way to bigger and better things professionally, and that meant bigger and better things materially. Now, Diane realized how little materialism really meant, how fleeting it could be, how fast it all could end.

She was suddenly distracted by a familiar sound. The car. She knew it by the powerful sound of its engine. Nobody in the neighborhood had one like it. The driver slowed down as he drove by, just as he had done so many times before. Diane hurried to the window. She pulled back the curtains and watched as the car was parked at its usual spot. The man was always smart enough to arrive and park when it was too dark to see his license plate. And other than the car being black, Diane wasn't knowledgeable enough about cars to identify it by make or model.

He would know she'd be watching. She was aware of that. She also knew that once he gave her time to get to the window, he would slowly pull away and, in a few minutes, there'd be another phone call.

But then she caught a slight movement in a doorway not far from the corner. Difficult to see at first, it was a figure, a man's figure. It eased out and slowly approached the car. She could tell from his motion that there wasn't a sound as he eased pat the rear of the car.

It was Joe's policeman. He didn't waste any time getting a man there. *Now, maybe this all might end,* she thought. But her thoughts were shattered by a noise that sounded like that of a drummer's heavy rim shots. Tat! Tat! Tat! The shadowy figure spun, staggered toward the driver's door and fell to the ground, on his back. The car door was opened. The policeman was trying to get up. Someone stood over the struggling figure for a few seconds. Diane could barely make out an arm extending toward the policeman. Then reddish-yellow flashes, in concert with four more explosions, again shattered the silence. Diane screamed.

Still gripping the curtains, she pulled them down and over much of her body as she stumbled backwards and fell across her bed. The door burst open. Diane fumbled for her gun. Bennett jumped to one side, her 45 gripped in both hands. "Don't shoot," she yelled. "Diane, what's wrong?"

"He's down there," Diane screamed. "He's killed a policeman." She grabbed her robe and raced past Bennett and toward the front door. Bennett followed.

The car was gone. Diane knew it would be. She reached the man. A stream of blood seeped slowly toward the gutter. It was like a miniature volcano flow as it carried tiny pieces of flesh and dirt with it.

"Oh, God," Diane cried as she knelt.

Bennett finally caught up, not too far ahead of other people who had enough nerve to venture toward the scene. They stared at Diane, kneeling by the body with a gun in her hand. While some stopped dead in their tracks, others quickly turned and retreated.

"It wasn't her," Bennett shouted as she turned and moved toward them. Then everybody retreated and some began to run. Bennett then realized she, too, was brandishing a weapon. The only thing she could think of was to yell that she was a police officer and needed help.

"You," she shouted to the closest of the onlookers. "Get to your phone and call the police. Now!" she screamed.

The person backed off a few steps, and then raced toward his home.

Diane was still kneeling beside the man. She was back on her heels, rocking slightly, her head buried in her hands. Her sobs were uncontrollable.

"Joe?" Bennett whispered.

Diane shook her head.

Bennett knelt beside her. There wasn't anything either could do. The man was dead. A bullet had ripped his jaw apart. Another had penetrated his neck. Judging from the amount of blood that covered the surface, it had severed his jugular vein. The rest penetrated his torso, the exact locations hidden by the clothes he wore. During those seconds, Diane wondered what mother or wife's entire life would change drastically just as hers had done. She wondered what this man's last words or thoughts might have been during those few seconds that Latsky hovered over him.

Chapter 25

By the time Spinaldo arrived, the area was already cordoned off. Policemen made sure the neighbors, who had returned, stayed at a distance.

Diane and Bennett were taken to a cruiser to await Spinaldo. When he arrived, he moved them to his car. "You guys alright?" he asked as he held the door open and ushered them into the rear seat.

Bennett nodded.

"Yes," Diane whispered.

Then he slid onto the front seat and faced them as best he could. "God, I was worried sick when I got the call. The officer who called me only knew two women were involved." He waited a few moments before continuing. "I know it's been tough, but can you fill me in on what happened?"

Diane described the incident from the time she heard the car. She stopped several times in order to calm herself. It was difficult, especially when she tried to describe what it was like when she reached the victim. She wasn't able to finish, and Spinaldo let it go. He knew what it was like, having been through the same thing enough times. No need to make it any tougher on her. They sat in silence for a while.

Spinaldo closed his eyes and slowly shook his head. "God, I probably should have had more men here," he muttered, lifting and moving a hand as though he didn't know what to do with it, then finally letting it fall to his lap.

"Damn. I really didn't think the guy would show, not after he was aware that we knew who he was. All my man was supposed to do was to try to ID Latsky. The only time he was to make an attempt to take him was if Latsky left the car and was heading toward your house. We knew that identifying him would be difficult in the darkness, but if he thought at all that the driver was Latsky, then he was to take the make and license number of the car, and call and wait for backup.

"Hell, it could have been some poor sucker with his girlfriend, unlucky enough to park in that spot. If that was the case, some innocent guy might have been shot as he stepped out of the car.

"We had several cruisers in the area that could have been here in a minute or two, surely not much longer. They could have blocked the car off and we'd have had him. Instead, it looks like Fred wanted to take the man alone. He knew better. It was a stupid and a costly mistake. It gave Latsky time to escape. Maybe it was my mistake for having Fred here alone."

"Maybe your man thought Latsky was going to leave and he could stop him," Bennett offered.

"But he was told not to do anything unless Latsky was heading your way. With Latsky's record, I didn't want one person tackling him alone. That's why Fred should have gotten the make and license number. Damn, that's what I told him, the make and number. Our cruisers could have run the guy down in minutes. This son of a bitch is smart, cunning. From what you told me about him and the neighborhood where he grew up, he's streetwise, knows all the moves. No telling how many scuffles he's had with the law.

"He had to know that we'd have some kind of a stakeout. Somebody else would have never shown his face, but for him, he's full of hate, and it was a challenge. But it was actually easy. The way I see it, and from where Fred ended up, Latsky probably watched Fred sneaking up on him from his mirrors, two sides and one interior. It was like a panoramic view of the area behind the car. With help from the streetlight, it was easy to watch Fred, who should have known better. He never had much of a chance. His gun's missing, so that indicates he had it out and Latsky took it."

"He just makes everything looks so easy," Diane muttered.

Spinaldo shrugged. "Seems that way, doesn't it? But really, Fred made it easy." He took Diane's hand. "Wait here. I'll be back. I don't want you going back to your home alone."

They were glad to comply. They watched as he and others roamed through the crowd, looking for any kind of witness or information that would help. After another hour, he returned with a uniformed policeman whom he introduced.

"He'll stay at your front door. We will have a continuous watch from now until this schedule thing is over. No, until we nail this guy."

It was a few minutes after four-thirty when they returned to Diane's house.

"It's like a nightmare. I almost can't believe it really happened," Diane said with a sigh.

"But it did, and that guy is worse than those people in Chicago said he was," Bennett said. She motioned both Joe and Diane to the sofa, and retreated to the kitchen to make coffee. After she served it, Spinaldo issued instructions.

He wanted blinds drawn over every window for the rest of the night and throughout the following day. He asked for a hammer and a few nails, than fastened the back door to the jamb.

"Now, there's only one way in," he said, "and with a man on guard at the entrance, you'll be safe. I'm using a uniformed man so that cruising police, from a distance, won't mistake a plainclothes man for Latsky and start shooting up the place.

"I'll be back to stay with you this afternoon until Latsky makes his move tomorrow. So I'll be here by dinner time today and I'll be staying."

He went to the porch. "Do not leave this porch for anything," he told the policeman as he stood in the doorway. Then he turned toward the women.

"Keep your guns handy at all times. Don't leave each other's sight other than bathroom calls. And then the other one stay close by. Sounds silly, but stay close."

The last warning, 'stay close' rang another long-forgotten bell with Diane. She later told Bennett how an uncle, who had been a fighter pilot, once chatted with her about air combat formations as they watched a war movie. He described how staying close to each other, a wingman he called it, provided extra cover against enemy planes.

"So, that's us, I'll be your wingman," Bennett said.

Diane checked the time after Spinaldo left.

"What a night!" Bennett said as she sat down on the sofa. "I don't know about you, but I've got to get some rest. And screw the blinds."

Dianne had no choice other than to squirm into the easy chair. No way was she going to be alone in a bedroom.

"Thanks a lot," she moaned.

"You're welcome," Bennett answered.

It seemed as though Diane had just closed her eyes when they were awakened by the sound of the doorbell.

"Now what?" she moaned as she checked her watch. It was nearly ten a.m. She and Bennett sat up, reached for their guns, and stared in silence at each other for several seconds, unsure of what to do.

"What the hell, the cop's out there," Bennett finally said. "It's gotta be him or we'd hear a commotion."

"This is the police officer. I'm sorry to bother you, but I've been here a long time. Can I use your bathroom?"

Bennett chuckled as she peered through the peephole at the distorted face.

"Poor soul. We can't let him dribble in his pants," she said. They assumed their positions and she unlocked the door.

The officer started in, then stopped abruptly in the doorway. Diane wondered why he stood perfectly still, when a few seconds before he had to go to the bathroom so badly. Her curiosity was satisfied in another second. Latsky, clean shaven, and in a two-piece suit, but whom Diane recognized immediately — he couldn't hide the huge scar — moved quickly behind the policeman from the side. He wrapped his left arm around the officer's neck and, with the other hand, held a gun to the man's temple. He pushed the man in and kicked the door shut with a foot.

"Go ahead," Latsky said, "use your guns. Go ahead. Shoot. Mine will go off by reflex, and you can wipe this clown's brains off the walls."

"Oh, God," Diane muttered, her legs already starting to melt. Her gun hand shook almost uncontrollably. "Not again," she moaned.

"Yeah, bitch, again." Latsky laughed. It was followed by his usual hacking cough. He spat a glob of phlegm on Diane's floor. "Just put the guns gently on the floor and kick them toward me. I'll count five and if you stupid bitches, who thought you could outfox me, haven't done it by then, goodbye brains."

Diane looked to Bennett and then to the police officer. His pleading eyes told her what to do. Latsky began counting. Diane placed her gun at her feet and pushed it toward the men. Bennett did likewise. "That was smart," Latsky said, as he pushed the policeman aside and motioned them to move further away. He picked up the weapons and put them in his pockets.

"You're providing me with a pretty good arsenal. What is it now eight, ten?" He laughed hysterically, as he took a step toward them.

The police officer moved toward him. "Look, why don't you just give me the gun?" he said. "Why do this? You won't get away with this. There are police all over the area."

"Here's why," Latsky answered. He faced the officer, smiled, and then shot him point blank in the face. The back of the man's head exploded, scattering skin, hair, brains and bone matter halfway across the room.

Both women screamed. Diane looked at the carnage, then to the front of her dress. It was splattered with the man's blood. She slumped to the floor in a dead faint. Bennett fell into the easy chair. She shook uncontrollably, pressing her hands over her chest. She tried desperately to catch her breath. Her heart was pounding. Latsky grabbed her by the hair and yanked her upright.

"Cut that shit out," he screamed. "Where's all the smart-assed talk now? Get your ass out to the kitchen and bring back some water and do it fast." He waved the gun toward the kitchen with one hand and pushed Bennett with the other so hard that she slammed against a chair and crashed to the floor. The pain was excruciating, but she was too frightened to cry out. She crawled a few feet, then scurried to her feet, rubbed her thigh where it had struck the chair and stumbled toward the kitchen.

"Oh, God, oh God," she muttered.

"Too bad, bitch," he yelled after her and laughed. "Maybe you'll move when I say so. And don't try bustin' out or Diane gets it just like the cop did. And move. We've got to get the hell out of here. If a cruiser gets here before we leave, then you both die a day early."

Bennett reached the kitchen sink just in time. She threw up. Latsky was screaming to hurry, and she had no time to even wipe off vomit that had splashed on the front of her blouse. She glanced at the back door and wondered for a fleeting second what she might have done had it not been nailed shut.

"Move yer ass or I'll kill both of you right now," he screamed. She hurried back. Water from a small pitcher splattered over her clothes. The man snatched it. She expected that he'd try to help Diane drink. Instead, he poured the water onto Diane's face. As she came to, he yanked her to her feet, and shouted: "Get your car keys, just the keys. Anything else and I'll mix your friend's brains with the cop's. And hurry."

Diane staggered to the table. She couldn't function. Her hands wouldn't follow her brain's directions. She fumbled in the purse but there was no sense of feeling. She was unable to tell one item from another. Things began to fall to the floor.

"What the hell are you doin'?" Latsky pushed her away from the purse. He emptied its contents onto the table and grabbed her keys.

"These?"

Diane nodded.

"Then let's get the hell outta here."

Diane knew neighbors must have heard the shot and prayed that the police would already be on their way. Even if they did call, there wasn't enough time. Latsky used Diane's car. In a matter of minutes, the three of them were out of the neighborhood. Latsky laughed. "A clean-shaven, well dressed man is far from what they're looking for. And you guys make one bad move, or try to signal anyone, and I'll blow your brains out. Understand?"

They didn't need to answer.

"Your husband made a bad move and I had to dirty up the inside of his car. And don't feel bad about the cop back there; he was gonna get it anyway. Couldn't let him sic his buddies on me. He was as easy as that jerk at the car last night."

Diane wondered how the officer at the door was duped into not questioning Latsky. It wasn't long before he answered without being asked.

"Dumb-assed cops." He laughed, then hacked and cleared his throat. "One's dumber than the other." He waited for either to ask why. When neither did, he laughed, then hacked again, cleared his throat, spit out the window, and continued. "Ya got a lucky neighbor. You like this suit? She provided it for me. Ya didn't say whether you like it."

"We do," Diane whispered.

"You're a lyin' ass. Ya didn't even notice it."

He ran his hand over his trouser leg and onto Diane's. She shoved it aside.

"That's okay for now. Later, I'll break your hand if you do that."

He turned east on to the Penn-Lincoln Parkway and remained quiet for nearly five minutes. Then he started laughing again.

"And ya didn't even notice how clean shaved I am. I guess you were too busy crappin' yer panties. I ain't as comfortable, but I had to be cleaned up in order to make my plan work. It was simple. I walk up to your neighbor's back door. That's why I ain't got a car. I'm dressed in a white jump suit like a repairman. I'm carryin' a toolbox. The lady answers the door, lets me in after I tell her I'm from the city water department. Then I shove a gun in her kisser.

"I take her upstairs. I ain't got time to screw around, so she gets me one of her old man's suits. It fit good enough. The thing that saved her life was that her kid comes in and looks at me, like who is this guy? But she stays real calm. Doesn't even shake.

"He's a friend, she says. He's a nice man. Then she sends the kid downstairs to play. It's about the first time in years anyone ever bothered to call me a nice man, and I guess she was hoping that I really was, so I decide that I would be. Ya see, I ain't as bad as you think. I stuff her in the closet and tell her I'll be stayin' around for a while, and if she makes one sound or leaves the closet, I'll shoot her kid's head off. I know damn well she ain't gonna move outta that closet for a week.

"I go to the kitchen, get a big baking pan, cover it up with tinfoil like there was some nice food in it. I walk out the front door and cut across the lawn toward your house. Hello there, I yell with a big smile on my face. The cop looks at me while I'm crossing the lawn from her house.

"Hi, don't shoot, I yell to the cop still smilin' like I'm jokin' about bein' shot. I'm John Sebastian, her neighbor, and my wife, Anna, made some good ole German apple strudel for Diane. I told Anna I'd drop it off when I leave for work. We know how Mrs. Duval must feel, and thought this and some hot tea might pick her spirits up. Maybe you could hand it in after I leave.

"Dumb ass smiles. What harm can a neighbor do? So he says, okay. I get there. He reaches for the pan. When he has it in both hands, he realizes how light it is, but by that time I have my rod out and I end up beside the doorway, while he tells you he has to piss. You know the rest. Pretty good, huh?"

Neither answered.

Chapter 26

After leaving Diane and Bennett, Spinaldo returned to his apartment, took a short nap, had breakfast and then headed to the police station. He hated leaving Diane and Bennett alone, but was certain they'd be safe with the back door nailed and the only entry guarded. Right now, he had other things to worry about, the most important of which was trying to run down Latsky before he could get to the women.

He pushed through the normal clamoring mass of humanity or sub-humanity, depending on who was describing it, and headed for his office.

"Where ya been?" his partner, Pete Zabala, asked as he pushed through the door.

"It was one hell of a night," Spinaldo answered. "I stayed with the women for a while. They were pretty frightened. Didn't get home till early morning. I had to at least take a cat nap, eat, and here I am, refreshed and ready to go."

"I'm glad you're ready to go," Zabala said, "because we are going."

"Where?"

"Jessie and Chuck found where the guy's stayin'. They played a long shot and, believe it or not, he's at the same dump where we found the husband's car. They figured he might have had a favorite whore up there. Talk about dummies returning to the scene of a crime. Well, anyway, they called. Haven't heard from them since."

"When was that?"

"Couldn't have been too long ago. The secretary told me when I got in a few minutes ago."

"Did you try checking with them?"

"Called a couple times, but no answer."

"Did it ever occur to you that they might be in trouble?"

"What could I do? Didn't you hear me? I just got here a minute or so before you did. So now you know as much as I do."

"Yeah, right. I'm sorry. They probably tried to take him alone. One of them should have called us, or the police up there for a backup and waited. If he was going to leave, then they could have tried to take him. I think we have some real dummies around here. We've already lost one person who didn't call for help. What people don't understand is this guy we're after is pretty damned smart. He's a street-smart, dumb-looking, screwed-up psychopath."

Spinaldo used the siren and sped on the Penn-Lincoln Parkway through Pittsburgh. He wished it were a parkway all the way to Greensburg, but once out of Pittsburgh's suburbs, the road changed to two lanes, and traffic was heavy. It would have been too dangerous to keep the siren on and the same speed, and it took well over an hour to get to the motel. The sign was the same, letters still missing.

Spinaldo muttered. "Strange, I don't see the guys and the place looks deserted. Business can't that bad. I'd bet on that. According to the policeman I talked to, I don't think this place would ever be shut down. Something's gotta be wrong." he said as he turned into the entrance.

"Oh shit," he muttered, as soon as they entered the compound. Two bodies were sprawled out in the parking lot, not far from an open door to one of the rooms. He slammed the car to a halt and they ran to the bodies.

"It's Chuck, and he's dead," Spinaldo said, as he knelt over one of the bodies.

"Jesse here, and he's gone, too," Zabala called. "Good Lord, his heads almost gone." He turned and threw up.

"Get back to the car and call the Greensburg police," Spinaldo shouted. He looked toward the entrance of the motel parking lot. "There's Chuck's car. Give them a description of Latsky, and that he has two women with him and we don't know the make of his car or the direction in which he's driving. Then call our people. I'm gonna talk to the manager."

Spinaldo hurried to the office. He expected the worst. Otherwise the manager would have called the police long ago, or come out when they arrived. He was right. There were two bodies in the office. One was slumped over in a chair in front of a television set that was still on. The other was sprawled just under an exit sign at the rear of the room.

"Almost made it," Spinaldo said out loud, then called out for the manager, but he knew there'd be no answer. The same man he had talked to before was on the floor behind the counter. It was difficult to tell where he had been shot but it made no difference.

"Holy hell," Zabala muttered as he entered and viewed the scene. "Didn't anyone hear any of this?"

"I'm sure they did. What ever whores and customers who were here heard it all," Spinaldo replied. "And they all locked their doors, propped chairs, beds or anything else against the doors real fast. As soon as Latsky took off and they were sure he was out of sight, this place emptied out like a house on fire. No telling who was in those rooms. Maybe even some of the local gentry who, in no way, would want to be found here. So there are no eyewitnesses ready to help and those who did see first hand ... well, are dead. And I'll tell you one more thing. We're going to find at least one more body, and it'll be in that room with the open door — Latsky's girlfriend. He wouldn't leave witnesses." Spinaldo was right again.

"Why hadn't anyone noticed the place was so empty?" Zabala asked after the police arrived.

The motel was well beyond the boundaries of the town. It was sparsely occupied all day long, maybe three or four cars at the most. But like most motels of that sort, business picked up after dark. The state and sheriff's people usually handled any problems, but there were very few.

"We'll get an APB out right away," one of the policemen said. "The wall undoubtedly prevented anyone driving by from seeing the bodies," Zabala said, "and you know damned well that if anyone arrived for business and saw that mess, they'd back out of there like a cat covering shit. They'd have no way of knowing if whoever did the shooting wasn't ready to ambush them. And besides some of them, dead or alive, wouldn't want to be identified."

They spent a half hour at the scene and then waited at the station to see if the police found any trace of Latsky. Spinaldo was more than restless. He paced the floor. He was anxious for word about Latsky, but more so to get back to Diane. He was just about ready to suggest they leave, when a Greensburg patrol car arrived.

An officer told them an unmarked police car was parked a couple miles east of here with a note in it. It read "thanks for the loaner." He handed the note to Spinaldo.

"For some reason, that bastard took Chuck's car. Do you know what that means?" Spinaldo asked nobody in particular, then answered the question himself. "It means that Latsky ditched that car knowing it would be recognizable, and some poor sucker, probably from this city, is in a ditch with a hole in his head, and Latsky is driving his car."

Spinaldo turned to Zabala. "Let's get back. There's nothing else we can do here and with this guy loose, I want to get back to the women just a fast as I can. You take the other car. I'm going directly to Diane's house. I'll be there for the rest of the day and tomorrow."

Chapter 27

When they left Diane's house, Latsky took the Penn-Lincoln Parkway east. Diane remembered the route. It was the same one Spinaldo took the day they visited the motel.

No one spoke. Occasionally Latsky would utter a short laugh, but neither woman had any desire to question what he was thinking about. A little over an hour later, they passed a sign that read: "Greensburg, Five Miles." Diane began to sob.

"What's that for?" Latsky said.

Diane didn't answer.

"Answer me," he screamed, "or I'll bust your head."

She screamed back. "You should know, you rotten bastard. Greensburg's where you killed my husband."

"Bullshit." He laughed. "Your husband was dead long before we got to Greensburg."

Bennett, sitting in the back seat, gave Diane's shoulder a slight reassuring squeeze.

At that moment, Diane swore to herself that Latsky would never have the pleasure of torturing her and then killing her. She'd kill herself some way or other, first.

She stared out the window. There was little to see other than signs, trees nearest the road, and an occasional house. Then another sign appeared: "Welcome to Greensburg."

"Oh, God," Diane moaned.

"Quit bitchin'. I'm tired of hearing about it, unless you want one across the chops. We're going on through Greensburg."

Diane remained quiet. She closed her eyes for most of the trip through the city, but couldn't help opening them as she sensed they might be approaching the eastern end of the town. She saw the sign, the motel office, but everything was dark. She wondered why. Then she caught a quick glimpse of a bright yellow strip of plastic tape stretched across the driveway. "DO NOT ENTER, CRIME SCENE."

"You see the sign?" Latsky said. "That's where I was before I visited you. Two stupid cops, who no longer exist, tried to take me. If they hadn't showed up, a lot of people would still be alive."

"What do you mean?" Bennett asked.

"Well, let me see. There were the two cops. Okay? Then there were two residents and the manager who saw, or at least heard what happened. They had to be taken out. And then there was the whore I was with. I don't like witnesses. That's six, right? I think some of those police asses should be getting the word that they can't keep up with me."

Diane or Bennett did not give him the satisfaction of acknowledging his comments.

A short time later, they began to climb up a steep grade, and Diane recalled from earlier trips east with her family when her father told her it was Laurel Mountain, the beginning of the western part of the Appalachian Range.

They reached the crest. On the right was a combined gas station and restaurant. On the left was a sign before a narrow dirt road that read: "State Game Preserve." Latsky pulled into the restaurant's parking lot.

"Listen," he said. "Bennett and me are going in. I want some cigarettes and beer. And Diane, you're stayin' in the car and not budging. If anything goes wrong, like you trying to escape, Bennett dies and anybody else in there goes with her. Understand?"

Diane nodded. She looked at the odometer and memorized the mileage.

They were gone only a few minutes, and then, Latsky drove directly across the highway onto the game preserve road. It was pitch dark. The trees, illuminated by the headlights, quickly approached and disappeared just as quickly into blackness. A deer, motionless after being momentarily blinded by the car's headlights, suddenly bolted and, with one huge leap, disappeared into that same blackness.

The road was a dead end. A log cabin was on the right and an entrance to the game preserve on the left. Latsky pulled up to the cabin. Diane looked at the odometer again. They had traveled one-and-one-tenth miles. She had no idea why she had looked at it at the restaurant, but now realized that subconsciously it might have been in case they were able to make a break. They would know how far it was to safety.

The cabin was sizable, made entirely out of roughly hewn oak logs. It had a flat, tilted roof and old-fashioned casement windows. Mud or clay was pressed between the logs. It appeared much like cabins in the colonial era. The center room was huge, serving both as a living and dining room. The kitchen at one end was open. It extended from the dining area. Thick doors leading to what Diane presumed to be bedrooms were at the opposite end. A bathroom, its door open, was between the two bedrooms. The builder had to go no farther than his backyard for wood.

"You'll like it up here," Latsky said, than laughed until he brought up another phlegm-clearing cough. He continued to laugh and cough. He said he was thinking about something funny.

"Yeah, it's funny alright, how I bought this place cheap from an old geezer recluse. Made him an offer he couldn't resist — cash — receipt and all. He liked the amount I offered, but didn't know I was going to pay him in lead. His new residence is on the south forty — a nice underground apartment. He's out there with some others, your husband included."

"You son of a bitch, you bastard, you're insane," Diane screamed.

Latsky brought the back of a hand across Diane's cheek. She slammed hard against a wall, then slid down into a sitting position, almost unconscious. Dazed, she managed to get to her feet, only to fall heavily back to the floor. She struggled into a sitting position, leaned against the wall, and tried desperately to shake off the sound of cymbals that were clanging in her head. She opened and closed her jaw several times. That worked. She ran a hand across her rapidly swelling cheek. It was numb — couldn't feel a thing. She looked at her hand. At least there was no blood. When she regained her senses, she agonized over the thought that it was nothing compared to what she and Bennett could expect.

"You might not make it through tomorrow if you keep that shit up," Latsky screamed as he stood over her. "My wife called me that just before I cut her throat." He stopped for a second, than continued. "So just sit there and keep your big mouths shut." He turned toward Bennett, but she quickly backed out of his reach.

He ordered Bennett to sit beside Diane, and spent the next few hours drinking beer. Every now and then he'd spew out some lewd remarks while fondling his genital area. That was always followed by loud laughs and hacking coughs.

"We're gonna catch some shut-eye, but I can't let you take a stroll," he said after finishing the six-pack. He went to a cabinet and brought back a spool of laundry rope.

"This'll keep you," he said as he tied their left arms together, putting the women into an awkward position. Then he tied the rope to his right arm.

"Now, if this rope pulls to the point where I think you got some wild-assed ideas about buggin' out, you'll find that slap was just a love tap compared to what you'll get."

The rope was long enough so that he was able to sleep on the bed with them on the floor beside it.

Diane decided that whatever transpired during the next day would probably not include sexual torture. That would come after midnight, leading into the sixtieth day and hopefully after they were dead, but she knew differently. It also meant that if they were able to find a way to escape before he started on them, chances were that they'd at least be in decent condition. She prayed that she was right.

Chapter 28

Spinaldo saw the multi-colored flashing lights from blocks away.

"What the hell's goin' on?" Zabala said when they reached Diane's house.

There were a number of police in the yard. Three police cars were parked in front and a yellow restraining tape was stretched completely around the house.

"Damn!" Spinaldo answered. "Something's happened to the women. Where in hell was the guard?"

They parked, stooped under the tape and hurried toward the house. A policeman stopped them.

"We're with you," Zabala said as they both showed their badges.

"What happened?" Spinaldo asked a nearby plainclothes man. "Where are the women?"

"All we know right now is that a police officer was killed inside. There are no women here. I don't know anything else. The problem is there are no witnesses. Neighbors said there's been so much going on over here lately, shots and all, that they're afraid half the time to open their doors. A woman next door called. She heard the shot, but she never left her house."

"Anybody in there?" Spinaldo asked a policeman.

"Yes, a couple homicide detectives. The head man's Jack Fletcher."

"Yeah, okay. We know him." Spinaldo turned to Zabala. "Fletcher was here when Fred Johnson was killed down the street."

"Good lord, " Zabala exclaimed as he viewed the blood-splattered wall and carpeting. "What the hell happened?"

Fletcher came from another room. He recognized them. "That's what we're trying to piece together. We noticed the rear door was nailed shut. And what the hell was that policeman doing here?"

"Why didn't you call me?" Spinaldo asked.

"Why? What do you have to do with this?"

Spinaldo had forgotten that only a few people were aware of what was going down and Fletcher wasn't one of them. And this was his territory.

"Where are the women?" Spinaldo asked.

"Women? What women. How many were there?"

"The neighbor just described the resident, Diane Duval. She was the dame who was with the cop down the street."

"Right. I know her. She had a friend, Marge Bennett, staying with her. What did the neighbor tell you?"

"She went through some shit, too," Fletcher said. "Some guy threatened her, then stuck her in her closet and dressed in one of her husband's suits. That's about all she knew. She heard a shot and called nine-one-one. They responded and found a police officer over there with most of his head missing. By the time the police got here, whoever did it was gone, probably with the women. The neighbor said she thinks they took Mrs. Duval's car. We identified the policeman from his badge number. He wasn't from our precinct."

"He was our man," Spinaldo muttered.

"Yeah? Well, like I said, why the hell was he here and if something was going down, why weren't we in on it?"

Spinaldo disregarded the second part of the question.

"I had him guarding the front door. Her life was being threatened. Four of our police officers have been killed in the last twenty-four hours at the hands of one guy."

"Four!" Fletcher exclaimed.

"Yeah. You were here for Johnson. Then two of my men bought it in Greensburg when they caught up with this guy. We found them in a motel parking lot when we went up there. Now this. When did this happen?"

"Early this morning."

"We must have passed that bastard on our way to Greensburg. He was coming back after the motel murders," Patterson said.

"Who in the hell is this guy you keep talkin' about?" Fletcher asked. "Come on, what's happening?"

"He's a maniac serial killer who is after Mrs. Duval and her friend. You can see by the nailed-up door and the policeman at the front door that we were trying to keep them safe. I wonder how the hell he did it, how he got the officer to let him in. That's three dumb mistakes and four lives lost."

Spinaldo grabbed Zabala by a sleeve. "Come on, we've got to get back downtown. I put a tracker on her car, and the receiver's in mine. If I had a half an ounce of brains, I would have driven my own car. That's mistake number four. We might have been able to tag him right away. With the guard, I just thought nothing could go wrong. The guy is really something. Right now, I'm hoping to hell that he's still within some kind of range."

"What about the women?" Fletcher asked. "Is he going to kill them?"

"Not yet. Not until tomorrow."

"What the hell does that mean? What the hell's going on?"

"Sounds goofy, I know, but I don't have time to explain right now, and I can't afford to lose any more time." He yanked Zabala's arm. "Let's get my car moving."

Zabala laughed as they drove off. "I know it's a hell of a time to laugh, but Fletcher's probably as confused as a milkman in a crematory. Every time you said something, it got more confusing for the poor guy."

"Yeah, I guess it is confusing," Spinaldo answered with a heavy sigh. "Fletcher's gonna kick my ass the next time he sees me, but like I said, we know how much time is remaining, he doesn't. And I'm not sure how the hell we're gonna track this maniac down."

Spinaldo sat back, trying to relax. It was impossible. Thoughts of what Diane and Bennett could be going through at that moment raced through his mind. He tapped Zabala's shoulder. "Stick the light out and move this damned thing."

Neither spoke for several minutes. Zabala noticed that Spinaldo was nodding his head as though agreeing with something he was thinking.

"What?" Zabala said.

"What's really distressing is that this bastard not only snowed the policeman guarding the door, but he's also snowed the hell out of me."

"How's that?"

"Here I am, here we are," Spinaldo said, "knowing that he didn't kill his victims until the sixtieth day, right?"

"Yeah."

"So I figure, okay, I'll get with the girls around dinner time tomorrow, stay with them for the rest of that day, and then straight through the sixtieth day. No way in hell was he going to get through me. Man, I talk about some of my cops being dumb. I'm worse than any of then. I planned to have men, even a SWAT team hiding all over the neighborhood, and nail his ass when he showed up. Like a jackass, I'm figuring he'll show sometime during the sixtieth day. And that wasn't even close. What I knew was that he was planning to kill them on the sixtieth day, and that's where I screwed up. What I didn't know was that he would come a day or two early and snatch them away. So he comes when nobody expects it, kills the guard and drives with them on the fifty-eighth day. We have no idea where they are. In just a little more than one day he'll start torturing them. And we have to find them before that. All we know is that he's holding them somewhere in this great state of Pennsylvania, and we don't have much time. That son of a bitch."

"Well, there's only one way to find him," Zabala said.

"Yeah, the tracker we had installed in Diane's car. That was a lucky move," Spinaldo said. "Let's hope it's working or that they're not out of range. That's about the only hope we have of ever seeing the women alive again. And I'll tell you one thing for sure, he's gonna tell us where to find them after he's done and the scene will not be pretty."

Zabala parked beside Spinaldo's car. They both sprinted to it. Nothing. There was no signal.

"Damn," Spinaldo muttered. "They're either out of range or this thing died. Now what?"

"Well, the only thing to do now is to pull ourselves together," Zabala said. "Let's go inside, grab a cup of coffee, put our selves into his place, and try to figure out where he could possibly be. Maybe if we guess close and the damned buzzer's working, we'll pick up the trail. Right now, unless someone spots Diane's car, there's not much more we can do."

"I'll take the coffee. I need that," Spinaldo replied. "But, I can't stand sitting around. Right now I'm going to start driving around this city, and the suburbs to see if we can pick up a signal."

They drove for several hours. Skipping the more affluent areas, they concentrated on older and more suspect locations: East Liberty, Homestead, Hazelwood, Greenfield, the Hill District and the North and South Sides. They checked continuously with the station. No word.

"What the hell are we doing? They could be in anywhere," Zabala said. "If the buzzer isn't working, we could have passed them up in any one of those places. It's panicksville, almost eleven o'clock, and we haven't even come close, and my eyes are burning out of my friggin' head."

"So, what are you suggesting?" Spinaldo couldn't think straight. His mind was cluttered with thoughts of Diane and Bennett and how those other women were tortured. "What the hell. Do you think you have something better than what we're doing?"

"Anything's better than just driving around in circles and getting nowhere, other than totally frustrated. What I'm suggesting is that we go back to the station, and eat something. I'm starvin', and like I said before, try to fathom where this guy might be holed up. What else can we do, except to keep driving around like two lame-brains? The way we're going, it could take another week to cover half of Pittsburgh."

As much as he hated to give in, Spinaldo conceded the futility of continuing what they were doing. They started back to the station.

"Another thought," Zabala said, "is that we should get at least a couple hours of shuteye. If we do get a break, we'll find out right away, and I don't think it's gonna do us or the women any good if we are so beat that we're useless. Let's just go into the lounge and get some rest. I'll tell the desk sergeant where we are and when to call us."

Spinaldo reluctantly agreed, but he had a difficult time and envied Zabala, who dozed off immediately. It seemed he had just managed to doze off himself when the sergeant awakened them.

"That helped," Zabala said.

Spinaldo complained that they had slept too long.

"No, we didn't," Zabala argued. "We're at least fresh, and that might mean a lot later on. Who knows?"

They ordered a breakfast from a nearby deli.

"This helped, too," Zabala said after wolfing down three eggs, bacon, pancakes and coffee in record time. "Now we might be able to think more clearly."

Spinaldo agreed.

"You know," Zabala continued, "we've been barking up the wrong tree, driving all over creation like fools. Think about it. If I was him, would I be hanging anywhere around here? Hell no. I'd be as far away as I could be."

"Maybe so."

Both men were quiet, trying to determine where they might hide out if they were Latsky.

"Wait a minute," Spinaldo said. "If I didn't get so panicky I would have thought of this long ago."

"What's that?" Zabala asked.

"He isn't from Pittsburgh, so he can't really know a lot about the city. That means he'd probably want to stay somewhere that's at least somewhat familiar. Diane said Latsky talked about a wooded area when she had him opening up a bit on the phone. So contrary to what I thought at the time, her conversation has helped. Think about it for a second. Where'd we come from this morning, and where has he hung out?"

"Damn," Zabala answered. "Greensburg or at least that area. And I'll bet you're right. See what I mean about trying to figure things out instead of going off in all directions like idiots?"

"It's a long shot," Spinaldo said, "but it's about all we've got. And there's plenty of woods around there too."

"Long shot, my ass," Zabala said. "That's got to be it."

"Well, what are we waiting for?" Spinaldo took a last hasty sip of coffee as he pushed his chair away.

Chapter 29

Diane managed to check her wristwatch while hardly moving the rope. It was after ten a.m. and Latsky was still snoring and snorting. Diane and Bennett had been awake for at least three hours. Sleep was nearly impossible during the night. They were uncomfortable to begin with and afraid to move without yanking the rope. And with opposite arms tethered, they suffered severely from cramps all night long.

"Sounds like a pig, doesn't he," Diane whispered.

Bennett nodded. "Acts like one too. What are we gonna do? Time's running out."

"I don't know, but we still have the rest of today, so the best thing is not to panic. We've got to figure out some way to outwit this imbecile, and if we panic, that'll never happen. We've got to keep calm and try to keep him off guard no matter what. Maybe Joe will find us."

"You gotta be dreaming," Diane said. "Face it. Nobody, including Spinaldo, has the slightest idea where we are."

"What the hell are you whispering about?" Latsky yelled, yanking the rope hard enough so that each of the women cried out in pain. "You heard me. What were you whispering about?" He yanked the rope again.

"If you must know," Diane said, almost belligerently, "we were wondering when you would wake up. Lying here like this for hours has been very uncomfortable."

"No shit," Latsky answered, laughing and followed by his usual hacking fit. "That's just too bad. What the hell, you ain't got but about a day anyhow 'till you find out what being uncomfortable really is. And I know you're figuring out how you're gonna bust outta here. But I'll tell you right now, either one of you makes a wrong move, I'll start early. Now you," he continued while loosening the rope and pointing to Bennett, "get your ass over to the stove and make some coffee and something to eat."

Bennett complied, and Latsky tied them to a leg at the far end of the table while he wolfed the food down. They sat on the floor with their plates in their laps. They had no knives or forks.

"Eat with your hands. You bitches, always telling someone how to act, how to eat, how to do this, and how to do that. You ain't fit to eat at the same table as me. And you better enjoy it because it's almost your last meal."

He tipped his chair back after he finished eating, opened his mouth and forced out a loud and exaggerated burp.

"You ain't a bad cook," Latsky said, while rubbing his stomach. "Too bad you won't be around much longer. I could use more cookin' like that."

He moved to an easy chair and looked at their plates. The food was untouched.

"You ain't eatin'. Don't you like your own cookin'?"

Neither answered.

"Ya know, I don't think I've ever had the chance to talk to any of the others about their hubbies. You see, I got to them right on schedule, and there wasn't any chance for them or me to sort of chat. You're my first ones I've had as guests to talk to."

Neither responded.

"What the hell's the matter? Don't you want to know how your husband got it?"

"No."

"Well, I'm gonna tell you anyway. The poor bastard was just trying to be a nice guy. You know, I always watched my guys for a long time. I do that to all of them. Got to know when they usually went out, and when and where they went to work. Learned their whole routine. I tailed your old man, found where he stopped on his way home now and then. That was usually at a grocery market, and I made my acquaintance there, just like a real nice guy. Bumped into him one day and apologized.

"Then I made sure to meet him there a couple times and struck up a conversation now and then about weather or a game. I got to know him and the others from that stupid, useless mail we got at the Gulf. He probably figured I lived in the neighborhood. Then when I was ready, I waited until he stopped off to shop again. So he's seen me shopping a couple a times, and we talked. I was such a nice guy." Latsky laughed, coughed and hacked.

"Then I tell him this time that my car went haywire, and wondered if he could give me a lift, just for a few blocks to my house. I even gave him the name of one of your nearby streets. He knows the street. He knows me now. So he gives me a lift. To make a long story short, the gun goes in his side. We pull into an alley. He tries to fight. The gun goes off. I drive here and I plant your husband in the south forty. No problem at all. Wanna go see?"

Diane didn't answer. Neither did she show any emotion. She'd be damned, she decided, if she would let him see her cry, or let him have any satisfaction from her mental and emotional anguish.

Latsky shrugged. "I thought at least you'd care."

"You did me a favor," Diane said and laughed. "I despised my husband." That had to be one of the most difficult things Diane ever said, but she was determined not to provide Latsky with any added pleasure.

It was different with Bennett. She was sobbing. "How could you?" she cried.

"Whatta ya mean, 'how could I'? I just told you how I could. It was easy."

Latsky started for his bedroom, laughing on the way as though what he had described was a big joke.

"Somehow, I'll get him," Diane growled. "Somehow."

When he returned, he was naked. He stood over them, as close as possible without touching them.

"Like what you see?"

Diane held her head back as far as it would go. *You bastard*, she thought. "You're the ugliest person I've ever seen. And you aren't even a man. You're inches from my face and you can't even get excited. No wonder your wife hit on another guy. If you're gonna kill us, do it now and get it over with. You're useless otherwise. From what I can see, you're not even a part of the male species."

"Diane," Bennett pleaded in a whisper.

"Don't Diane me," she shouted. "If he's gonna do it tomorrow, why not do it now and get it over with? Why not?" she shouted at him.

Latsky slapped her. When she fell back, Diane yanked heavily on the rope. Bennett came down on top of her. Their arms dragged against each other. Both yelled in pain. Latsky laughed, and then surprised them. He helped them back into a sitting position.

"I'll do it when I'm ready, you bitch, not when you're ready. And I'll be good and ready after midnight. That'll be number 60, in case you've forgotten. Yeah, and we're gonna have fun. Regardless of what you might hope, those broads weren't dead before I worked on them, and neither will you be. And neither was your mother, so think about that for a while."

He pushed Diane's head hard against the table leg. By the time she regained her senses, Latsky had returned to the bedroom.

"Are you crazy?" Bennett whispered.

"No," Diane answered, trying to rub away the throbbing at the back of her head. "I knew he wouldn't do anything now. Maybe beat up on us a bit, but I was hoping that it might get him a little off guard. Who knows? Maybe he'll get careless. Besides, I was furious. God, I thought he crushed the side of my face.

"One thing, Marge, if you think I'm not scared down to my socks, think again. If we can't get away, then we've got to figure a way to kill ourselves, because I'm never gonna let him butcher me while I'm alive. I'll fight him until he kills me. Then, it won't matter what he does. But until then we have more than fifteen hours to figure a way out."

They sat in silence. It wasn't long before Latsky returned, fully dressed. "I'm gonna leave you dear little piggies for awhile, but don't get excited. I'm just goin' for some more beer, and don't think you're gonna get away." He untied the ropes, ordered them to their feet and pushed them toward the bathroom. "You'll stay in there until I'm ready for you to cook my dinner. And don't dream of breaking out. That door is twice as thick as those you're used to. Too bad your mother didn't have a door like that." He laughed, coughed and than spat into an ashtray.

"Maybe while I'm gone, you can decide what you'd like for your last meal." His laughter echoed throughout the room as he pushed them into the bathroom, locked the door and propped a chair against the handle. "That'll keep you safe and sound," he yelled. "I'm taking my truck, but don't get excited. I'm also taking your keys."

Spinaldo kept the siren on at full blast and weaved through traffic. He almost ended up in collisions several times as some drivers, seeing lights and hearing the siren, moved over to the berm, while others, not as alert, kept moving on the macadam.

"Holy hell, Joe," Zabala yelled. "Ease, up man. I want to get there alive, okay?"

"And I want to get there fast," Spinaldo answered. "And that's what we're gonna do. No telling what's happening to the women already."

They were but a few miles east of Pittsburgh's suburbs when Zabala nudged Joe.

"Do you hear what I hear? And it isn't a Christmas carol."

Spinaldo cocked his head. "What?"

"Listen."

"Damn, man, it's the beeper," Spinaldo said. "Than they did come this way."

"Yeah, but do me a big favor, don't go any faster. If we crash, we won't get to wherever that signal's coming from. We're too close now to screw up."

Spinaldo nodded.

Then just as quickly as they heard the signal, it disappeared. Spinaldo pulled off the road.

"There's not a turnoff road in sight. What the hell happened?"

Zabala shrugged. "I have a SWAT team buddy," he said, "who's familiar with these gadgets. Sometimes they aren't too reliable, he told me. They can die or get jarred loose. He also said sometimes they die out due to certain surroundings, and then come back in again. There are tons of hills and woods around here that could interfere, so maybe we should just keep going. Not much else we can do."

The signal returned shortly before they passed through Greensburg. The motel was dark.

"They'll clean up the blood and be back in business in no time," Zabala quipped. "I'd like to blow the frigging place up."

"There's one thing you forgot to do," Spinaldo said, as they passed the entrance.

"What's that?"

"Look for Diane's car in the lot."

"Damn."

"Never mind. I did. No dice. I thought he might be arrogant or whatever enough to bed down in a motel where he just committed a half dozen murders."

The signal continued strong. They reached the base of Laurel Mountain and a bit later, the restaurant at the crest. The signal sputtered off and on.

"Probably these damned woods and the power towers across the street," Zabala said.

Spinaldo pulled into the lot and looked for Diane's car. As he walked toward the door, looking backwards into the lot, he bumped into a man who was hurrying out. He juggled two six-packs of beer, almost jarred loose from the force of the impact. Spinaldo apologized. The man didn't look up and didn't answer.

"Now, what the hell do we do?" Bennett said. "He's got us locked in here until it's time to kill us. Oh God. Oh God," she moaned, almost crying.

"Damn it," Diane yelled. "Stop that now! You're the one who talked about all of your hair-raising experiences. So don't start falling apart on me now. Get that damned lucky bullet out, and start rubbing it. Maybe you'll come up with an idea on how the hell we can get out of this."

"There's no way. No one knows where we are. We're locked in this room. It's almost day sixty and Lazlo's drooling at the mouth thinking about what he's gonna do to us. Spinaldo's sixty or seventy miles away and this bastard will be back to finish the job and move on to do the same thing to others. What chance do we have?"

"I don't know. But as long as we're alive, there's always a chance. So let's look around."

"Look around? Where? Have you forgotten where we are, stuck in a tiny bathroom? There's nowhere to look and nothing here but a sink and a commode."

"And a medicine cabinet," Diane said, as she opened the mirrored door. "Let's see what the hell's in it."

She began removing its contents and calling out the items as she laid them on the top of the commode's water tank, as a nurse would do while lining up instruments for an operation.

"Adhesive tape, old fashioned razor and a box of blades, tooth brush, mouth wash, and judging from that bastard's breath, it isn't his, rubbing alcohol, after shave lotion and some prescription medicines. Not much to work with," Diane muttered. "But maybe."

"Whatta you mean, maybe, and not much to work with? I don't see anything to work with."

"That's because you have a reporters imagination — just the facts, just the facts. If the facts aren't there, you have nothing.

Bennett, now use your head. Years ago I read a book about gangs in Brooklyn. It was called *The Amboy Dukes*. My father had it in his library. The Dukes and other gangs learned how to make home-made weapons among which were guns — they called them zip guns — and knives they called shivs. So, this is a start."

"For what?"

"For making a Duval top of the line model shiv, and hope and pray it's effective."

Diane took the toothbrush and taped two razor blades, one on each side of the brush end, but opposite the brush.

"See, a shiv. It will be good for one slash," she said, "so we'll have to make it good."

"That little thing?" Bennett mocked. "What good will that be against a gun or a deranged giant?"

"Don't kid yourself. This little thing could zip your jugular with not too much effort."

"But how do we get to his?"

"That's a dumb question. I don't know how we get to his, but at least we have a weapon in case we try."

"Oh God, we don't have a chance."

"If you don't shut your mouth, I'm gonna try out this shiv on you. What the hell's wrong with you? I'm the weak little house-wife and you're supposed to be the tough reporter. Isn't this a role reversal? Quit your bellyaching and help me out."

"How? There's nothing more in here other than a stupid tin wastebasket."

"How stupid? As a matter of fact, that's a smart wastebasket and you're smart for thinking about it."

"Come on, Diane, it's no time for comedy."

"Comedy, hell. Nothing is funny now. I was so scared when he came back out of the bedroom naked that I thought I was going to crap my pants, and things haven't changed since. I'm scared silly, but at least you've given me another idea." Diane emptied the basket and placed it in the center of the room.

"What's that for?"

"A mixture."

"A what?"

"A mixture. A mixture!"

She filled the basket halfway with water.

"Now you can turn around or watch, but I'm going to make that bowel movement I said I almost made when Latsky came out of that bedroom."

"A bowel movement?"

"That's what I said, a bowel movement, and its going right into this can instead of the commode, and then you're going to do the same."

"Are you crazy?"

"No, but right now consider me as crazy as Latsky. Crazy has to beat crazy, and that's exactly why this might work."

"I'll turn around."

Diane finished. "Now, it's your turn."

"I can't."

"Like hell you can't. You'll do it or I'll kick you in the ass and set your butt on the can myself."

"Turn around."

Diane turned and waited.

"Okay," Bennett whispered after a few minutes. "How humiliating."

"How humiliating will it be when Latsky sticks a knife where you just relieved yourself? That pain would be nothing compared to what might be in store for us. Okay," Diane continued, "open all those bottles — alcohol, the medicines, everything and start pouring it into the basket.

After that was done, Diane turned a plunger that was stored behind the toilet upside down and stirred the concoction.

"God, how revolting," Bennett said.

"Good, I hope Latsky thinks so, too."

Diane placed the can on the toilet lid.

"Here's what we do. And if you chicken out, it's very simple, we die. We've got to do this together and no screw-up. Understand?"

Bennett nodded. She was shaking, her hands almost twitching.

"Settle down. That's what I mean. You can't do that when we have to make our move. When he comes back, we've got to coax him to open the door right away. As soon as he does, I'll throw this in his face. Hopefully, some of it will get into his eyes. The smell won't be any different than what he's used to, but I'm banking that it'll surprise the hell out of him. Then I'm going to swipe at him with my little shiv, and as soon as I do that, you push the bastard as hard as you can. We race for the door and pray like hell it isn't locked. Than we head as fast as we can straight for the woods. They're right across the road, if you remember. So don't turn right or left when we go out that door. Go straight ahead. When we're in the woods, we go left and run like crazy. Hopefully, we'll outrun him for the mile to that restaurant. And than we hope there's someone there who can help us, preferably someone who owns a gun. Now that's a lot of hoping and a lot of luck, but what else is there?

"I'm also hoping that if we don't make it, one way or another, I'm going to force the bastard to shoot us, and we'll still avoid the tortures that he has planned for us. Once we start, there's no hesitation. Got it?"

"Yes, but I hope he hurries. The smell is getting to me."

"That's yours, not mine," Diane said and giggled.

Minutes seemed like hours as they waited. Finally, they heard the car outside. Diane closed her eyes, tilted her head back and released a long stream of air as she listened to the pebbles in the driveway crackling under the car's tires.

"Here we go," Diane whispered. "You ready?"

"Yes. I'm ready for another movement, that's how scared I am."

Diane picked up the can. She held the bottom with one hand, the top with the other.

"Don't get in my way when I toss this junk."

"Don't worry about that."

"Hey, bitches, I'm back," Latsky yelled as he entered. "Did ya miss me?"

"No, but I knew it was you before you spoke. I could tell by your dog-shit smell," Diane yelled defiantly, hoping that he'd get mad enough to open the door. It worked.

"I'll let you out, you slut. Than I'll tell you just what I plan to do to you."

"Oh God, God, God, God, God," Bennett moaned.

"Shhh. We cannot cave in now." Diane held the toothbrush by her teeth.

The door handle rattled slightly as Latsky removed the chair. He swung the door open and started in.

"Okay, you —"

That's as far as he got. Diane tossed the mixture as high and as hard she could. It hit Latsky squarely in his face. Then she threw the can at him and slashed out with the razor knife. She knew she cut him somewhere. His first yell of surprise was followed by a scream of pain and then curses. Diane started for the door and Bennett followed up perfectly with her assignment and shoved him hard as he tried to clear the concoction from his eyes and wound. He toppled backwards over the chair he had just removed. His head collided heavily against a bedroom doorjamb.

As Diane raced past the kitchen table, she spied a gun, quickly scooped it up and continued out the door. Bennett was close behind.

Latsky's screams and curses echoed throughout the house as they raced off the porch, across the road and into the dense underbrush. They had a decent head start since it took time for Latsky to get to his feet, clear away the debris from his face and find a weapon.

It was odd, considering what was transpiring, that both women would laugh as they reached the woods. But for a few fleeting moments they did. It was a combination of the release of the fantastic tension that had intensified with every second they waited, and the joy — as fleeting as it might be — of realizing that a plan, which had such a slim chance of succeeding, was actually working. But it was just the beginning.

They ran as fast as they could, stumbling and falling, helping each other up and encouraging each other to keep going. Thorns and thistles pierced their arms, legs and faces as they ran and stumbled. Low-hanging branches punished their upper bodies, sometimes entangling them like a trap. Berry bushes, low to the ground, wound around their ankles, virtually tackling them and sending one or the other, face first, into the next prickly plant. The pain, not only from the falls, but also from the thorns penetrating their hands, arms and even their faces as they ran and tumbled, was agonizing. There was no way they could keep quiet, no way to stop the gasps. It was like radar for Latsky, who they could hear for fleeting moments whenever they reached a rare clearing. He cursed as he, too, stumbled, but he was gaining ground, and it left Diane and Bennett no time to consider pain. Escape was the only thing on their minds.

Bennett yelled for Diane after falling into a thorn bush. "I can't go on."

"Like hell you can't," Diane yelled, as she yanked Bennett out of the bush and onto her feet.

At that moment, some fifty yards behind, Latsky caught a glimpse of them and fired two shots. The bullets weren't even close, but the ricocheting sound assured both women that they could go on, and pain was of no consequence.

Chapter 30

"Be with you in a minute," the man behind the counter said as he picked up a tray of food and headed for a table at the rear of the room. He spent several minutes bantering with the patrons. It seemed like an hour. Finally, the man returned, and Spinaldo showed his badge.

"We're looking for some people and we think they're up here somewhere. We're thinking that maybe somebody here, maybe you, may have seen them."

"I just got here, so I can't help you, but I'll call the boss. Maybe he knows. He's back there doin' the cooking."

Spinaldo paced the floor. Two minutes later, just as an impatient Spinaldo was about to go back to the kitchen, the owner pushed through the swinging doors.

"Sorry for making you wait, but in this business, our customers have to come first." He offered them a drink. They declined.

"We're looking for some people that may have come up this way. A man, big, maybe a bit gruff looking, and two women. Probably yesterday or last night."

"Yes, I remember them," the man replied. "But there was only one woman. I was even thinking at the time that she looked kind of uncomfortable. He bought some beer and cigars and left. He's been around here off and on for a few months. As a matter of fact, strange that you should ask about him because he just left a few minutes ago. Bought a couple six-packs."

"The guy we bumped into," Zabala exclaimed. "Son of a bitch, right in our hands."

"Do you know where he might have gone?" Spinaldo asked.

The man escorted them to the front door and pointed toward the dirt road.

"There. He goes back that way whenever he leaves. There's a cabin back there."

"Where's the road go?"

"Nowhere in particular. It leads to the entrance to state land. It dead-ends. An old timer owns a cabin back there. Come to think of it, he hasn't been around for a while. He used to come in at least once every four days or so."

"How far to this guy's place?"

"To a dead end. It's a little more than a mile. I usually take the old guy food whenever he is sick."

"It's him all right. If the women are still alive, we've got to make sure they stay that way," Spinaldo said.

"If 60 days was correct, we've still got about eight hours, I sure hope they are alive he's kept to his routine."

They drove slowly to avoid anyone hearing them and parked some distance from the cabin.

"It's Diane's car," Spinaldo whispered as they rounded the last curve in the road. They drew their weapons. Spinaldo motioned Zabala to the opposite side of the yard, and on his signal, they started toward the cabin. They were brought to an abrupt halt by the sound of two shots.

"The women! In the woods!" Spinaldo yelled.

"Damn," Diane cried, "the bastard's gaining on us. He's like a bear, plows right through this stuff."

She held Bennett by the hand. They weren't even halfway to the restaurant. Fighting the bushes, falling, getting up, running, falling again, and repeating the cycle over and over was rapidly sapping their strength and endurance.

"Come on, we can't stop now," Diane urged, knowing that she, too, was just about at the end of the line. She stumbled and dragged Bennett down as she fell. Latsky was closing in. Both women struggled to their feet and staggered on. It was fear, not strength that kept them going. They reached a small clearing and a fallen tree trunk.

"Sit for a couple seconds and take deep breaths," Diane said. "He's got to be tired, too."

"No more" Bennett said, gasping and barely able to speak. "I can't go on. You go. Let him shoot me. Like you said, it'll avoid the torture."

"Damn it!" Diane yelled. "You've got a book to write. Now get off your ass, and let's get outta here."

"I'll try," Bennett managed, as she struggled to her feet. Two shots rang out. Bennett gasped and tumbled backwards over the log.

"Oh, no," Diane cried out as she climbed over the log and knelt beside Bennett.

Latsky was within thirty yards, fighting his way through a thick patch of underbrush. He was laughing hysterically.

"Oh, God. It hurts," Bennett moaned.

Diane put her hand over Bennett's mouth and whispered as fast as she could.

"Turn onto your stomach." Diane helped her. "You've got to be absolutely still and quiet. Latsky has to think you're dead. He's very close, so you must bear the pain. No matter what happens, don't move and don't make a sound. I'll continue on, and seeing you down, he'll continue after me, I'm sure. When he does, you've got to get up and get as far away as you can. Do not worry about me. I'll be all right."

With that Diane got up, ran another ten or fifteen feet, then faced Latsky, who by then, had broken through the bramble patch. He was closing in, still hysterical.

"She's dead, you bastard. You've killed her," Diane screamed.

"And you're next," Latsky yelled as he slowed to a walk. "You dumb bitches didn't think you were going to get away from me, did you?" he bellowed. "I have my gun and my hunting knife, so I'm gonna finish the job here and now. I'm gonna kill you, but not right away. I want you to feel the pain from the bullets smackin' you in different places. Then, while you're still alive, I'm gonna skin your ass and hang it up on a tree. And you can yell and scream all you want, which you'll do. But I'll be the only one who will hear, nobody else. And it'll be fun listening. Too bad your friend won't be able to hear it."

He raised his gun and pointed it toward Diane. She knew she had lost, and it wouldn't be but a second before she'd begin living through the worst torture imaginable. She waited for the explosion that would also abruptly deprive her of carrying out her last wish.

"Stop," Spinaldo yelled.

It surprised both Diane and Latsky. He spun around.

"Who the fuck?" he yelled and fired a shot blindly, then turned again toward Diane.

A shot rang out, another, and another. All missed their target.

"Fuckin' people can't even shoot straight. But I can, and you're history." Latsky again pointed his gun at Diane.

More shots, and one caught him in the right shoulder. His arm dropped limply, and the gun fell out of his hand as he fell to his knees. Latsky staggered back to his feet. Screaming and cursing, he stumbled toward Diane.

Throughout the whole ordeal, the running, tripping, falling, the brambles and thorns, Diane had somehow managed to hold on to the .357 Magnum she had snatched off the table, and she suddenly realized that it was her own. Because of pain alone, she should have dropped it long before as she stumbled through the forest. But subconsciously or otherwise, maybe even by luck, she held onto it.

Then everything came together in a flash. There was no hesitation, no fear, and no words like "not again." The training by

Sergeant Felts on how to use that particular weapon resurfaced during those fleeting seconds.

She had promised herself, and Latsky, that the next time there would be no panic. And there wasn't. She was perfectly calm.

"Diane, don't," Spinaldo yelled, as he fought his way through the bramble patch.

Nothing. Nobody was going to deprive Diane. She held the .357 with both hands and aimed, just as Felts had taught her. It recoiled halfway to her face as it exploded. It bounced back, and she pulled the trigger again.

The impact knocked Latsky backwards. He struggled to his knees. His buttocks rested on the back of his calves. His expression was blank, unbelieving. He stared for a fleeting second at Diane. His expression spoke, said it all, without a word. He pressed both hands against his chest. The huge soft-tip slugs penetrated that part of his body neatly, but tore his back to bloody shreds as they exited. He raised his hands to his face and stared in disbelief at his blood-drenched palms. He tried to scream, to curse, but the expletives never left his mouth. The words and thoughts — his last — were abruptly denied, just as he had denied so many others. He fell forward on his face. He was dead.

Diane dropped the gun just as Spinaldo reached her. She slumped heavily into his arms. There was no remorse, no sorrow, only a feeling of profound relief. After what seemed like an eternity of fear, there would be no more screaming, no more phone calls, no more threats, no more chases. It was like the forest, that minutes before had been so threatening, so uncompromising. It was now safe, serene.

It was over.